Two L

Lauren Willig

This is a work of fiction. Names, characters, and incidents are products of the author's imagination or are used fictitiously and are not to be construed as real. Any resemblance to actual events, locales, organizations, or persons living or dead is entirely coincidental.

For my mother,
who likes this book best.

With many thanks
to Dean Kagan, Professor Hay,
the Winter Writing Program, and the HLS class of
2006,
without whom (and which)
this book could not have been written.

CHAPTER ONE

"...In time the rod
Becomes more mocked than feared; so our decrees,
Dead to infliction, to themselves are dead,
And Liberty plucks Justice by the nose;
The baby beats the nurse, and quite athwart
Goes all decorum."
        --<u>Measure for Measure</u>, I, iii, 26-31

Griswold Hall squatted like a toad in the middle of campus, a non-descript building in an inconvenient location, so squashed against its neighbor that it was an endless puzzle to incoming students where Griswold Hall began and Areeda Hall ended. Even if the student were to succeed in locating the correct door, tucked away beneath a coarse stone lintel and a large tree, the interior of the building provided a landscape as welcoming as the Minotaur's cave. The glass doors gave on to a platform stranded between floors, leaving the entrant faced with an unappetizing choice of up or down. Below, a dark cavern of maroon brick, possibly the basement, possibly the first floor. Above, more stairs, leading to an unseen landing. It was enough to daunt any but the most determined petitioner.

On the second floor, safely tucked away above the labyrinth of stairs, a man stood by a window.

One arm was propped against the windowsill, his head tilted downwards in the classic expression of pensive melancholy. His mood was as perfectly fitted as his J. Press suit, tailor-made to suit the occasion and his frame. His tie was a somber maroon, dotted with a series of small shields that subtly indicated to those who knew that he had matriculated at the same institution over which he now presided. His hair was gray, but it was the gray of Hollywood and successful politicians, the perfect accessory to a J. Press suit, like the chrome fittings on the hood of a Mercedes.

From the hard-won harmony of his office, the Dean gazed down on the path that spanned the length of his domain, bisecting the law school campus in a wavering line, like an incision made by a surgeon with a twitch. From Pound Hall, the path meandered past the gleaming glass of the International Law Center, paid homage to the stately nineteenth century brick of Hastings Hall, and veered away from the defensive huddle of Griswold and Areeda, forcing the walker to wander as it wandered, to twist and turn as it twisted and turned.

There was no symmetry to the campus, no logic to it. Buildings had been plunked down with glorious disregard to the style and situation of their fellows. Langdell Library, as coldly classical as a founding father, turned its back on the bulk of the campus, presenting its elegant front to a quad consisting of buildings belonging to other faculties, an estranged patriarch giving the cut direct to its offspring. Griswold and Areeda huddled in the lee of the library, modern and ashamed of it, while Pound Hall, like an aging activist who hasn't yet realized that the bell bottoms and tie-dye went out with the Summer of Love, smirked at the top of the rise, the exposed strips of concrete and broad expanses of glass that had once been so avant-garde, so daring, now as quaintly dated as Austin's gothic arches, and a good deal less durable. The concrete was crumbling and the windows leaked.

It was, thought the Dean, not an inappropriate landscape for the study of the law, full of dead ends and blind corners, a hodge-podge of disparate precedents forced into conjunction and called a whole.

Below, class had just let out. Clusters of students moved in gusty surges down the walkway, each to their own kind. 1L's, huddled in their protective herds, trudging under the combined weight of casebooks, cribbooks and computers. 2Ls, strutting with all the confidence of their completed year. Even the odd 3L, an exotic beast on campus, heading with gym bag straight from the mailboxes in Harkness to the newly refurbished machines at Hemenway Gym, with never a stop at a classroom in between.

From the window, the students presented a study in skin tones. Tanned shoulder blades stuck out above the low square backs of tank tops; pale flesh, like uncooked dough, surged between too-low jeans and too-short shirts. Painted toenails protruded between the thongs of flip-flops, and whippets of wind proved to the curious viewer that the waxing salons of Harvard Square were well employed while the law school was in session. Only the men were fully clothed, from the

3

baseball hats on their heads that shadowed their faces to the trailing laces of their sneakers.

As the Dean watched, one boy swaggered past the gym, disappearing into a little saltbox house that looked more like the home of an early American writer than a school building. In that simple, white-painted frame house, generations of America's finest legal minds had mulled over the great questions of the day. Future Supreme Court justices and Solicitor Generals, senators and statesmen, they had burned the midnight oil, debating policy and precedent, agonizing over interpretations and slaving over citations to uphold Harvard Law Review's proud reputation of excellence.

The Dean glanced sideways, to the cluttered surface of his desk, where the latest copy of the Law Review, proud product of a summer's work, awaited his perusal.

It was only forty pages long.

This latest issue of America's premier legal journal had been set in type designed to eke out as many pages per character as possible, the margins wide enough to satisfy a medieval monk with a yen for extemporaneous illumination. The table of contents listed a mere three articles, all by assistant faculty, and one "note" by a member of the Law Review staff. The note dwelt lovingly on the rise of internet poker tournaments. There might be a dearth of citation—and, indeed, law—but no one could deny the enthusiasm with which the piece had been written. The author had clearly spent a great deal of time studying his subject.

From the walls, past law school classes gazed with varying degrees of scorn and boredom at the anemic efforts of their successors. Young men in spectacles with slicked back hair, wild-eyed radicals with beards and placards. All were gone, pressed flat as flowers between the pages of a yearbook, leaving behind them a wilderness of bared flesh and barer minds.

Through the pale wasteland of flesh, a darker figure darted through, a crow among doves, making purposefully for the entrance to the library. Oh, they were still there, thought the Dean. The idealistic, the studious, the curious minds waiting to be filled with precedent and policy. But they were the few, not the many. The call of the library presented no challenge to the strident blare of Lincoln's Inn, the law school's coyly named frat house.

"It's no good, Chaz," the Dean said wearily.

The Provost joined him at the window. "I don't know, Will. I think they look pretty good." From the vantage point of the second floor, the wonder bra had never done its job more effectively.

"That's exactly what I'm talking about."

"You can't very well expect them to live a monastic existence. We want them to emerge well-rounded individuals, versed in all the experiences life in Cambridge has to offer. A lawyer must live life before he can regulate it."

"Don't quote the catalog at me, Chaz. I wrote it." Wrenching the shade shut, the Dean propped himself against a corner of his desk. "It's all gotten out of hand. Too much excess, too much self-indulgence... just too much."

The Provost cast his old friend a dubious look. "Are you saying we shouldn't have given them the free coffee?"

"It's not just the free coffee. It's not even the ice skating rink."

"You're not going to get rid of the masseuse?" asked the Provost, with real alarm. "My sciatica...."

It had all begun so innocently. The free coffee. The ice skating rink. The masseuse. Every innocuous step on the road to academic disaster.

When the Dean had taken over the position from his predecessor, five years back, Harkness Commons, the student building that housed cafeteria, lounge and mailboxes had last been renovated in 1952. The mailboxes were crumbling; the walls were spotted with food and damp; the murals, so bright and cheerful during the Korean War, were flaking off the walls in large chunks, bits of paint and plaster falling into the students' soups and salads like improbable croutons.

And it wasn't just the physical condition of the school. Morale was as low as the water-logged ceiling. Students scurried between library and dorms in a never-ending rerun of "The Paper Chase," working themselves into nervous disorders along with their clerkships. A general air of gloom, thicker than the sludge of a Cambridge winter, pervaded the campus, spurring the Yale Daily News to print a series of triumphal editorials ranking Harvard Law lowest among law schools for personal satisfaction. When Dean Arden took his place in the office on the second floor of Griswold, applications were flagging, donations were dropping, and the faculty were suddenly discovering a deep-seated desire to return to the world of private practice. The only thing that was rising was the suicide rate.

Something had to be done. The students weren't socializing enough—so he rebuilt the plaza in front of Harkness Commons, putting in little tables and awnings in the fond hope of replicating a Parisian bistro.

But they were still listless. Coffee at the Hark cost over a dollar a cup, and tasted like mud, to boot. In fact, the Dean wasn't entirely convinced it wasn't mud. Goodness knew there was enough of it in Cambridge, miring the walkways, clogging the drains, trickling through the cracks in the Gropius dorms. So he brought in free coffee, in big black urns, and placed it at strategic junctures throughout the main classroom buildings.

The coffee, everyone agreed, was splendid. But they felt so jittery, so tense. Too much caffeine, combined with the stresses of work....

So he had hired a masseuse, just for 1L exam period. Then the 2Ls complained. Their schedule, after all, was just as grueling, made more complicated by the hectic search for a job. Weren't their shoulders tense? Didn't they deserve a little backrub? Rebellion brewed in the Faculty Lounge. Forget the 2Ls' job search, they were the ones who had to teach the ungrateful little brats, not to mention the grueling drain of being on constant call by the media. All those book tours, and media appearances, and celebrity trials... it was enough to drive the most stoic of scholars into a decline.

By the end of a week, the masseuse was on permanent call at the gym, with a sub-staff of four masseurs in training, and a side-line in pedicures.

He had inherited a campus of cloistered nerds, quivering with neuroses. Five years later, they were caffeinated, they were massaged, they had free alcohol on Fridays, and wide-screen televisions in their dorms. The workload had been cut and the student activities fund had been raised.

In short, he was running the country's most prestigious summer camp.

"Your sciatica is safe from me," said the Dean. "Have you seen this?"

With one neat motion, the Dean flicked his copy of "The Record" across the desk. The paper fell open to a grainy photo of a couple standing in front of the bulletin board at the Brattle Theatre. Their linked hands had been highlighted with a thick, black circle. *Lecturer's Love Tryst with Student!* the headline ran.

"Unfortunate," said the Provost, shaking his head. "You would think he would have better sense than to be seen in public with her."

"I'm going away," the Dean said abruptly.

"Away?" The Provost's balding head was still buried between twin wings of newsprint. "For the weekend?"

"For the rest of the term." The Dean pushed off his desk, forestalling further questions. "I'm appointing Arthur Agnelli as Acting Dean."

"Agnelli?" The Provost dropped the paper. "He's an excellent scholar—no one doubts that—but isn't he just a little bit too...."

"Idealistic?"

"Don't you mean unrealistic?"

"That," said the Dean, "is exactly why I want him."

"But, Will," remonstrated the Provost, "don't you think that might not be a mistake? Remember what happened at that faculty meeting...."

"You mean the one where he suggested mandatory expulsion for any sexual or academic infractions?"

"First offenses, Will!"

"That's one way of making sure there won't be a second."

Even if they were regularly enforced." Agnelli's pointed glance spoke of an old argument.

"That sort of problem," the Dean said cheerfully, "is precisely what I wanted to talk to you about. I have a proposition to put to you. One I hope you'll like. Chaz is all for it, aren't you, Chaz?"

The Provost mustered an unenthusiastic thumbs-up. "Sure thing, Will."

"What is it?"

"I," said the Dean, "will be going away for a bit. It's unavoidable, I'm afraid, and very hush hush. You know the sort of thing."

"Iraq?" A tinge of interest lightened the long lines of Agnelli's face. "There was a rumor about a commission...."

"That would be telling. Where I'm going isn't important; it's the school that's important, and I want to know there's a good hand at the helm while I'm away. Not just a good hand, the best hand. Your hand, Arthur."

The Dean could see prudence warring with desire in Agnelli's expression; it quivered through the bridge of his nose, straight down to his lips. "There are others with more experience...."

"But none with your reputation."

Fairness forced Agnelli to say, "I don't have any administrative experience."

"How can you say that? With this sitting right here!" The Dean gestured towards the five hundred closely typed pages of Agnelli's proposed revised disciplinary code. "And look at the way you've run the Women's Studies Center—"

"The Center for Studies Regarding Women in the Legal Professions," corrected Agnelli stiffly.

"—for the past five years. A tour de force, Arthur, a veritable tour de force. I'd like you to turn some of that force to the law school as a whole. Just think of the good you can do. Think of the changes you can make."

A sound akin to a groan emerged from the otherwise silent provost.

"The antacids are on the desk, Chaz. What do you say, Arthur?"

"I do have a few ideas…."

A private smile spread across the Dean's face. "I rather thought you would. I wish I had time to hear all of them, but there are preparations to be made before I leave."

"Of course," said Agnelli courteously. "If I can be of any assistance?"

"Oh, you already have, Arthur. You already have." As the provost wrenched the cap off the little tube of antacid tablets, the Dean clapped Agnelli on the back. "Can you be ready to take over by Monday? I'll provide you with a list of routine tasks, of course, and anything that I forget, Mrs. Dexter will be sure to remember. She's been on the job longer than I have. But mostly," he added, in a confidential tone, "I want you to take whatever steps you feel are needed."

"Any steps?" inquired the Provost weakly, popping another tablet as the masseuse and her clever hands shimmied inexorably away.

"Almost any," replied the Dean jovially. "Nothing too wild. We don't want the alums up in arms."

"You mean," said the Provost, "you don't want donations to drop."

"Without those donations, there would be no cure for your sciatica."

The Provost lapsed rapidly into silence. It wouldn't do to call Agnelli's attention to the presence of a masseuse on staff. With any luck, he wouldn't notice.

"Well, Arthur?" asked the Dean. "Are you up for it?"

Agnelli's eyes were fixed on the open copy of "The Record" on the Dean's desk.

"I believe I know where to begin," he said.

CHAPTER TWO

"The Duke is very strangely gone from hence...
...Upon his place
And with full line of his authority,
Governs Lord Angelo, a man whose blood
Is very snow-broth; one who never feels
The wanton stings and motions of the sense,
But doth rebate and blunt his natural edge
With profits of the mind, study and fast."
                    --I, iv, 50, 55-61

When her phone buzzed, Megan was in the library, seated beneath her favorite portrait of Christopher Columbus Langdell, founder of the Harvard Legal Method, and namesake of the law library.

Megan would have preferred to pursue her studies beneath the auspices of a woman, but the decoration of the library had not yet caught up with the advent of female jurists. Besides, the chair beneath the portrait of Elena Kagan was decidedly uncomfortable. The goals of feminism could better be pursued by concentration unbroken by the distractions of the flesh, especially the tender flesh between back and thigh.

Megan's phone buzzed again, earning her a dirty look from the boy seated next to her—a 1L, judging from the huge Civ Pro book and the general lack of personal hygiene.

Hitting the ignore button, Megan tried to concentrate on her casebook, but her caller refused to be deterred. The phone rattled embarrassingly against the polished wood of the long library table.

Squirming sideways in her chair, Megan flipped the phone open, and breathed into the mouthpiece, "Hello?"

"Meggy Meg Meg Meg!" caroled the voice on the other end of the phone. She thought the voice sounded familiar, but she hadn't heard it for some time, so it was hard to be sure. It sounded like....

"Gabe? I can't talk right now. I'm in Langdell."

"Easily solved, no?"

Last year, that air of easy confidence had been a challenge, even—she admitted to herself, in the sterile peace of Langdell—a turn-on. There was something very attractive about a rampantly unregenerate male chauvinist just waiting to be reformed.

Or, rather, there had been something very attractive.

"No."

"Awwww, come on." Without waiting for her assent, Gabe went on, "I need to talk to you about Cliff."

Megan's shoulders stiffened under her cashmere sweater. Gabe wasn't the only person who wanted to talk to her about Cliff. Since last Thursday, when the news broke, her inbox had been filled with emails from "The Record," "The Harvard Crimson," "The New York Times," and a series of other news organizations of varying creditability, all wanting the inside scoop on the latest scandal. Megan had deleted them all with a rapid-fire series of staccato clicks, and instructed her roommate Rachel to screen all calls.

When she signed up for the Board of Student Advisors, notoriety was the last thing Megan expected. Every year, a bewildered new crop of 1Ls came in. And every year, they would be broken into seven sections of about eighty students apiece. In the incestuous hothouse of their sections, they took all their classes, made friends and enemies, dated and broke up and dated again. Gabe, appropriately enough, had been a product of Megan's section the previous year.

But eighty people was still an unwieldy number, so, for First Year Lawyering, their required legal writing and reasoning class, the 1L's were broken down once again, into mini sections of ten students. And to each mini-section was assigned a wise—or not so wise, since there was no academic prerequisite for the position— 2L or 3L, who served as liaison between students and the FYL lecturer, grading papers, soothing wounded egos, and telling lying stories about how it would all get better. Really.

Megan had been thrilled to be assigned as TF to Harvard Law's newest lecturer, Cliff Walker. His Law Review notes, immortalized in the electronic archives of Westlaw, showed a sensitivity to the nuances of the law that would make for interesting discussions in teaching meetings. It also hadn't hurt that he had come straight from a clerkship in the Supreme Court with the very Justice Megan had her eye on.

It had been one of Megan's students he had been caught with.

Of all the eight mini-sections he oversaw, why did Cliff have to choose to date someone from hers? It shouldn't have felt like a personal slap in the face, but it did.

"Can't this wait? I have my Con Law reading to do, and ten FYL papers to grade for tomorrow."

Including Cliff's girlfriend's paper, sitting innocently in the pile with the rest. The ink ought to have blazed scarlet.

"Hell, no, it can't wait! The disciplinary committee is meeting Friday."

"That shouldn't be much of a problem for him." Against her better judgment, Megan powered down her computer, watching as the little paperclip man whizzed away into the distance, taking her notes on the dormant commerce clause with him into electronic slumber. "The Dean will find some way of getting him off. He always does."

"Unh-unh." Through the phone, Megan could hear the brush of the stiff bill of a baseball cap against the silver-coated plastic of Gabe's phone. "The Dean's gone."

"What?" Megan dumped her laptop into her canvas tote bag—all natural fibers—somewhat more forcefully than she had intended, wincing as it banged against her blackberry.

"Where have you been all weekend? Locked in a box?"

"Not where you were, that's for sure," Megan returned. "I was away at a conference in New Jersey, on the trafficking of women in third world countries."

From the background, "That's hot!" warred with, "Pick up any tips?"

"Who's there with you?" she asked sharply.

"Just the guys," said Gabe soothingly. "So you haven't heard about the Dean?"

Curiosity won over indignation. Hoisting her bag onto her shoulder and tucking her chair away neatly beneath the table, Megan abandoned a well-deserved lecture on the plight of women in third world countries in favor of a simple, "No. What happened?'"

"He's gone. Finito. Exeunt. Bye-bye. Auf wiedersehn. Adieu. Some top secret sort of mission."

"The Sudan?" exclaimed Megan, navigating around a couple canoodling at the head of the stairs. "At the conference this weekend, they were talking about setting up a commission to draft guidelines for the more humane treatment of—"

Gabe cut her off before she could go into detail. "No one knows. The point is, he's gone. And he's left Agnelli in charge as acting Dean."

"Agnelli? Professor Agnelli? Are you sure?"

"F-ing sure," said Gabe, with feeling.

"That's fabulous!"

"It's a disaster. Old Agony's going to come down on Cliff like a fucking armored brigade."

"It's no more than he deserves."

"Meg," Gabe's voice was gently reproachful. "How can you say that?"

"Um, let me think about it. He broke school policy and violated every possible set of ethical standards. What's not to come down on?"

"Right. Got you. Listen, the guys and I were talking—" In the background, Megan could hear a murmur of assent from the guys—"and we think you should talk to Agnelli on his behalf."

"You've got to be kidding."

"Would I kid about something like this? Oh, shut up." That last was directed, not to Megan, but someone in the background. The sounds of a scuffle reached her ears. Gabe re-emerged, somewhat breathless. "You TFed for him. You *know* the guy."

"So do you."

"Yeah, but I'm not the editor of the Women's Law Journal."

"The Journal of Women and the Law," Megan corrected by rote.

"Whatever. Old Agony likes that sort of thing. The point is, you have cred."

From the sounds in the background, the guys agreed. Either that, or someone had scored a touchdown.

"Gabe, where are you?" Megan demanded.

"In Gannett House," Gabe sounded wounded. "Where else would I be? We have a shitload of articles to edit. Anyway, that's my point. Cliff's not just a guy, he's a *dude*."

"He slept with his student, Gabe. *My* student. I don't care how much of a dude he is, there's no getting around that. I wouldn't want to get around that."

"Meg," Gabe was beginning to sound frustrated, "he was editor-in-chief of Harvard Law Review. Editor-in-Chief. Do you know what that means?"

"It means," said Megan, slamming through the door at the base of the stairs, "that he was complicit in strengthening the sexist stranglehold on the academic organs of the law."

"Have I mentioned how sexy you are when you talk theory?"

"Nice try."

"Look, it wasn't like she didn't want it. She's a big girl, she chose to go out with him. You should be supporting that. Aren't you always on about a woman's right to choose?"

Trust Gabe to take an interest in the wrong end of reproductive rights. "That's different."

"Un-huh. She knew him from before; they were the same age. Hell, it would be practically un-American to tell them they couldn't go out. Like Big Brother, or something."

"There can never be free choice where there's a power imbalance."

"You mean like your being smarter than me? Does that mean you coerced me into our relationship?"

"Good one, Gabe!" floated through the phone, followed by the cracking noise of a high five.

"I wasn't aware we still had a relationship," Megan said coldly. "Considering that the last time I actually saw you was, what? August?"

"I've been busy. The Law Review doesn't just edit itself, you know."

In the background, Megan heard strange scratching and whisperings, like the movements of very large mice. Megan had flashbacks to her early days in ballet class, and the dance of the Rat King from the Nutcracker.

"Which way are you walking out of Langdell?" Gabe asked abruptly.

Megan pushed through the glass door that led out of the passage that cut between the library and Areeda Hall. "The back way. Why?"

If he thought he could placate her with an eleventh hour appearance....

"Great! Paul is coming to meet you."

"What?"

"He'll go with you to see the Dean."

"I never said I would—tell him not to bother."

"Too late," said Gabe cheerfully. "He's on his way. Give me a buzz, and let me know how it goes, okay?"

"When am I going to—"

Megan found herself talking to a blank screen. Gabe had hung up.

"Hey!"

A stocky figure came pounding up the path, his Duke sweatshirt flapping in time with his panting breaths. Looking more like Barney Rubble than Barney Rubble had ever contrived to look, Paul skidded to a stop, his genial face flushed with the unaccustomed effort.

"Megan! Ready to go talk to the Dean?"

"Where in the hell is Gabe?"

Paul swung an arm around her shoulders, propelling her inexorably towards the sunken entrance to Griswold Hall.

"Don't worry about Gabe. He's busy. Real busy."

*   *   *

Every year, hundreds of anxious applicants applied to the Law Review. Locking themselves into their apartments, they spent a week cached away from the world, poring obsessively over citations, checking footnotes, writing long and esoteric arguments on topics bound to baffle the most dedicated of legal scholars. Some dropped out after a mere day or two, muttering distressedly to themselves as they dumped the thousand page contest packet into the recycling bin along with their ambitions. Others slogged doggedly through, barely sleeping, barely eating, seeking that Holy Grail of Legal Education: a Law Review editorship.

For those few, those happy few, their future was assured. Firm jobs, clerkships, tenure, all fell like golden fruit from the Garden of the Hesperides into the palms of the epic heroes of the Harvard Law Review contest.

There were some who dared to insinuate that the Law Review contest might, in fact, be rigged.

Such allegations were clearly nothing more than the mutterings of malcontents. The Law Review thrived, as it ever had, on merit alone, and it was pure coincidence that for the last five years the meritorious all happened to be members of the law school frat house. Malt does more than Westlaw can to justify the ways of the Courts to man.

In the basement of Gannet House, the mighty wheels of the Law Review had ground to a halt. Unedited articles littered the floor among a welter of empty pizza boxes, x-rated magazines, and the Sports pages of the Sunday Times.

On a pair of battered barca loungers, two of the Chosen were engaged in a far greater task than cite-checking. They were saving the world.

One X-box at a time.

"It looks bad for us if a Law Review editor goes down," said Dan, taking out his aggressions on a series of enemy entities. "It sets a bad precedent, you know?"

"I know," agreed Gabe, flinging his phone down next to his half-empty beer, and applying himself seriously to the task of wiping out Crushcon Five. "We might actually have to start going to class."

"Will she do it?" Dan pressed down hard on his joystick, sending an alien being flying into space. "Score!" he crowed.

Gabe pulled his baseball cap down lower on a head of dark curls whose carefully careless style would have made Lord Byron pale with envy. "Worth a shot. Better her than us."

"You know," said Dan, as his spaceship dove towards certain destruction against a rocky outcropping of space reefs, "I've always wondered. How did you wind up dating the editor of the Women's Journal? Fuck!"

GAME OVER blazed from his side of the screen.

Gabe shrugged, sending his own spacecraft soaring. "Nice boobs."

"A, B, or C?" Dan tossed the joystick aside and reached for the chips.

Gabe considered. "B, but perky. You have to consider quality as well as quantity in these things."

"What about quantity and quality?"

"In the law school?"

"Good point.

"I'm not stupid," said Gabe self-righteously, extinguishing an entire alien race with one flick of the wrist. "Just lazy."

*   *   *

"I don't know what you expect me to say," said Megan, hitching her canvas bag higher on her shoulder as they climbed the stairs to the second floor of Griswold Hall. "You know how I feel about this."

"No one twists words around quite like you," said Paul hopefully, trailing along slightly behind her. "Remember last year in FYL?"

"You mean when I rewrote your brief for you?"

"I really appreciated that."

"Uh-huh." That had been another Gabe special. The midnight phone call. The compliments. The wheedling. The "I'd really appreciate it if you would...." The five hours of formulating topic sentences and correcting citations.

This, Megan promised herself, was the last time she let Gabe talk her into anything. The occasional presence of a warm body on Friday nights just wasn't worth the hassle.

"Hi," Megan positioned herself in front of the Dean's secretary, a motherly sort with bobbed gray hair and a thick Medford accent. "Is Dean Agnelli in? If he's busy, I totally understand. No need to bother him."

Mrs. Dexter checked a paper on her desk and smiled at Megan. "No bother," she said cheerfully. "You're just in time for office hours. Go right on in."

"See," whispered Paul, poking Megan in the back. "I told you. It's a good omen."

"It's the end of my academic career, you mean," muttered Megan. "Agnelli is a monument in the field of Women's Legal Studies. The pinnacle of the field. His book—What in the hell was I thinking? He's going to hate me."

"He's going to love you." Paul gave her a little push. "The way we all do."

Making a face at him, Megan slipped reluctantly through the glass door of the office.

She had been to the Dean's Office once before, as part of a delegation to discuss the reform of the first year curriculum, standing with the others at they outlined their proposals for the replacement of the mandatory Property course (surely an antiquated notion) with one in Civil Liberties, and the substitution of interactive exercises for the Socratic method. Socrates, after all, had been both white and male, with a taste for humiliating his unfortunate followers.

Then, the cheap pine floor had been covered with a faded Persian rug, the sort favored by imperialist apologists and gentlemen's clubs where the crotchety subsided gently into that good armchair. The furniture had been chintz, arranged into small, conversational groupings, and the walls hung with class pictures, progressing slowly from the sepia smugness of blazers and bow ties to tank tops and baseball caps, interspersed with a series of inoffensive art prints. Not a one of them, Megan had noted, the product of a woman or a minority. Gaugin's representations of Tahitian women did not count.

Now, the Persian rug and class photos were gone, along with Van Gogh's daisies and Monet's water lilies. The chintz chairs had been replaced by a hodge podge of half-opened boxes, spewing books onto the bare floor. A series of hastily erected shelves, bolted haphazardly into the cheap plaster of the wall, were already filled with an eclectic collection of monographs ranging from law to political science, literary criticism to sociology. Framed photographs jostled for space next to untidy piles of scholarly periodicals, coffee-stained and frayed at the edges.

But it was the pictures that caught Megan's eye. Where the class of '55 had once hung, a beaming Gloria Steinem posed next to a very young-looking Professor Agnelli. He held a fishbowl; she held a bicycle. In large letters on the bottom, a decisive hand had scrawled, "To Arthur, who could almost teach a fish to ride." His bell-bottoms brushed the back wheel of her bicycle.

One photo over, an even younger Agnelli, with wild hair and a Che Guevera beard, surged at the camera waving a placard that read "ERA now!" The Washington monument loomed behind him, and in his other hand, clasped to his chest, Megan could just make out the title of a copy of Ruth Bader Ginsberg's "Sex Bias in the U.S. Code". The woman marching next to him, with the unkempt hair and the big sunglasses, surely that had to be Betty Friedan.

And there, below a blown-up photo of the unveiling of the Center for Studies Regarding Women in the Legal Professions, sat the man himself. His hair had been a touch longer in his placard carrying days, his skin less weathered, but the two were unmistakably one and the same.

Megan took an instinctive step back, in the grip of a case of hero worship as intense as a sore throat. She couldn't advocate Cliff's cause to Dean Agnelli; the entire idea was absurd. It would be like pleading with the Pope on behalf of Satan in the midst of a ring of holy relics.

The Acting Dean, the head of the Center for Studies Regarding Women in the Legal Professions, author of countless books and articles, hadn't seen her yet. He was on the phone, a droop of gray-streaked brown hair shading his eyes as he jotted notes onto a cream-colored pad. Recycled paper, Megan had no doubt.

Megan looked longingly at the door. She could just sneak out now, before he looked up. Mrs. Dexter would never say anything, or even she did, she didn't know who Megan was. Anonymity had never seemed quite so attractive.

Through the glass of the door, Paul gave her a thumbs-up, and jerked his head in the direction of the Acting Dean.

Megan pointedly turned her back on him.

"Sir?" she asked tentatively. "Dean Agnelli?"

CHAPTER THREE

"...When maidens sue
Men give like gods...."
        -- I, iv, 81-82

"Isabella: O, pardon me, my lord. It oft falls out,
To have what we would have, we speak not what we mean.
I something do excuse the thing I hate,
For his advantage that I dearly love.

Angelo: *We are all frail."*
        -- II, iv, 117-121

"Mercy is not itself, that oft looks so;
Pardon is still the nurse of second woe."
        -- II, i, 283-4.

"Yes?" Separated by nothing more than the width of a hand-loomed Peruvian rug, Professor Agnelli's voice sounded just as it had from a hundred different microphones in a plethora of university auditoria, low, well-modulated, with just a hint of something self-deprecating behind the vowels.

Megan realized she was twisting the strap of her bag and made herself stop. All the personal development seminars she had attended had been very clear about the importance of body language.

"I am so sorry to disturb you, Dean Agnelli."

"No need for formalities here," said the Acting Dean, rising. Coming around the desk, he held out a hand to her in greeting. "At HLS, we are all fellows in the same grand project. Call me Arthur."

Megan kept her cold hands circumspectly on either side of her pin-striped Banana Republic pants. "My name is Megan Milner. I'm a 2L."

"Milner…." The shadows under the Acting Dean's eyes seemed to deepen. "The name sounds familiar."

Megan had the unfortunate feeling she knew why, so she said hastily, "I'm on the editorial board of the Journal of Women and the Law, so maybe that's where you've seen it. I can't tell you how much I admire your work, sir. Especially *Legal Bodies*."

"Ah." Agnelli tilted his head in recollection, his gray-streaked hair flopping over his noble nose. "*Legal Bodies: The Objectification of Women in America's Leading Law Firms*. A modest little contribution to the field, but, I flatter myself, not a wasted one."

"I've read it ten times, and every time I find something I'd missed. There was that brilliant bit on unintentional biases within the hiring structure—"

"*The Length of Your Resume or the Length of Your Legs?*"

"The statistics on hiring rates for women who wore skirts to interviews versus those who chose pants suits was deeply eye-opening, especially the graph that indexed skirt length to GPA. I was very surprised by the way the hires all clustered around the middle of the graph, on both indices. I would have thought it would have gone the other way, in either direction."

"Smart but not too smart, short but not too short. The average is always less threatening."

"And then there was that wonderful chapter on the ways in which the timing of the legal day has evolved to subtly discourage women, with lots of long, late hours rather than a shorter, more concentrated workday."

"It is the insidious biases that are the most dangerous," reflected Agnelli sadly. "The ones so deeply imbedded in the system that we don't even notice them anymore. Or, if we do, we take them for granted as a necessary aspect of the overall structure. I believe the phrase often used is 'That's just the way things are'."

It was also the heading of his chapter, but Megan forbore to point that out.

"But you've shown that it doesn't have to be!" Megan took an impulsive step forward, into the ray of light that slanted through the uncovered window. "Your chapter on alternative models for the future of the law firm... it opened up a whole world of possibilities."

"With any luck," said the Acting Dean, moving back behind the bulwark of his desk and settling into his ergonomic chair, "with more students like you, someday those possibilities will be put into practice. Now, what can I do for you?"

With the official symbol of his authority once more between them, Megan felt her momentary confidence ebb. If she could have, she would have excused herself and left then. But the presence of Paul, squished bug-eyed against the glass of the door, spurred her on.

"In addition to the Journal of Women and the Law," Megan began slowly, wishing Paul, Gabe, and every member of the Law Review past or present to perdition, "I'm also a member of the Board of Student Advisors."

Across the piles of paper on the desk, the rough stone paperweights and the half-empty mug of green tea, she could see comprehension beginning to spread across the craggy planes of the Acting Dean's face. His eyes slanted briefly sideways, to a pile of newspapers occupying one corner of the desk, indicating that he just remembered where he had heard her name before—and in what context.

Megan deemed it best to get the rest over with quickly. "I was one of Cliff Walker's teaching fellows. Julia Kempe was in my section."

"So," said Agnelli, leaning back thoughtfully in his chair, "you've come to see me about our lecherous lecturer."

It seemed an unusually flowery flourish until Megan realized he was simply quoting from the bold lettering of the *Boston Globe* that sat on the desk next to the phone. Beneath it were similarly marked copies of *The Times*, *The San Francisco Chronicle*, the *Herald-Tribune*, the *Sun*, and even *The National Inquirer*. The *Inquirer* propounded the shocking news that Cliff was actually an alien, sent to populate the world with Martian lawyer-babies. "First our legal system, then the world!"

read the headline. Cliff's skin had been skillfully tinted a subtle green.

"You will, I am sure, be pleased to know that the appropriate steps are being taken. I gather that is why you came to see me?"

"Well... not exactly." Megan wished with every fiber of her being that she could partake of the joys of shared condemnation, instead of defending the damned. "Any relationship between a professor and a student smacks automatically of coercion. And Cliff must have known what the ramifications of his actions were. But...."

"But?"

From the walls, the founding mothers of the feminist movement gazed sternly down. Megan could feel their disapproval stinging her shoulder blades, like hail against a tent.

"But I was wondering if there might not be some mitigating factors for Cliff in this particular instance," Megan finished in a tangled rush.

"I fail to see what they might be."

The Acting Dean's tone did not invite speculation on the score. With an authoritative flick of his wrist, he closed a file that sat open in front of him—Cliff's file. Megan could only be relieved that her own wasn't within reach.

"I would be remiss in my duty to the school, and to the principles of the law itself, if I allowed so flagrant an infraction to go unpunished. The handbook," Agnelli tapped one calloused finger against that item in illustration, a small, sky blue book, with a blurry picture of Langdell Library on the cover, "clearly reads that 'no Law School faculty member shall request or accept sexual favors from or solicit a romantic or sexual relationship with any student who is enrolled in a course taught by that faculty member.' *Shall* not, Ms. Milner. Not *may* not, not *should* not. The drafters, remiss as they may have been in other respects, were quite clear on that."

"Right," said Megan. "Of course."

"Mr. Walker was a member of this faculty. He engaged in a romantic relationship with a student enrolled in his class. His actions fall squarely within the prohibited behavior."

"Of course. I see." Megan nodded vigorously as she backed away from the desk. "I'm sorry to have taken so much of your time."

"Not at all. Best of luck with your studies, Ms. Milner."

There was no warmth to his good wishes, just a courteous desire to see her gone. Mustering a tortured smile in reply, Megan hastily pushed back through the glass door, all but bowling over Paul in the process.

She would have continued straight on to the elevator, preferably to Gannet House, to commit indignities upon Gabe's person, but Paul blocked her path. The broadening effects of a keg a week made him a formidable obstacle, in girth, if not in mind. Which was, Megan realized, probably why Gabe had chosen him for the task.

"What the fuck was that?" Paul demanded indignantly. "If Cliff were on Death Row he'd be electrified already!"

Clamping her arm down over her tote bag, Megan tried to elbow past. "It's electrocuted, not electrified. And I did the best I could under the circumstances. It's not my fault Cliff got himself into this. You heard

Dean Agnelli—he falls smack into the language of the disciplinary code. There's nothing I could do."

"You call that advocacy?" Paul's dirty blond hair stuck up in all directions. "Even I could have done better!"

That stung. Megan had been witness to his lackluster performance in 1L moot court the year before. It was like being lectured about one's weight by Sally Struthers.

"It's your own fault!" retorted Megan heatedly. "I told you I didn't want to do this."

"But did you have to argue for the prosecution? Shit, Meg!"

"I—oh, the hell with it."

Turning, she stalked back down the hall, brushing her knuckles against the glass of the door in the ghost of a knock as she slipped back through, into the Dean's office.

"Dean Agnelli?"

"Arthur," he reminded her by rote, putting down the hand that had just been reaching for the phone. His greeting was considerably less effusive than it had been ten minutes before.

"I'm sorry to intrude on you—again." Megan grimaced. "But... does Cliff really need to be fired? No one disputes his guilt, but isn't there some sort of lesser punishment that could be levied on him? An unpaid sabbatical, or a year of teaching a basic 1L course, or something like that?"

She had committed the unforgivable error in judgment of speaking on behalf of the witches rather than the good townsfolk. Agnelli's expression was as implacable as Cotton Mather dealing with the Devil.

"I'm surprised to hear you ask that. Someone of your academic caliber."

"Cliff is a good scholar." That much, at least, she could say without flinching. "And it seems a shame to deprive the academy of the services of someone who has so much to offer."

"Too much to offer," Agnelli said dryly. "Judging from the report."

"But is that really our place to judge? The relationship of two self-determining individuals…."

"Is constrained by the same code of conduct that governs everyone at Harvard Law." Dean Agnelli's tone indicated that the discussion was over. He turned to the phone again, as though she had already gone. As far as he was concerned, she had.

With her reputation as well as Cliff's job hanging in the balance, sheer desperation lightened Megan's tongue.

"Isn't our legal system predicated upon the interpretation of events in context?" she burst out.

Agnelli's brows drew together beneath his shock of hair at this unprecedented act of lese majeste, but his hand stilled on the receiver.

"That's the very bedrock of the common law, the idea that every case must be determined in the light of its own unique fact pattern. Isn't that the first thing we're taught when we get here, that there is no black-letter law? No easy answers?"

He was watching her now, face as unreadable as an Easter Island statue. Megan's voice faltered a bit, but there was no choice but to go on, like riding a unicycle downhill.

"We have underlying principles, that guide us in our analysis, like the criteria on sexual harassment in the

HLS handbook," Megan plucked up the pale blue book, and waved it in the air, "but the application of those principles is always a matter of interpretation." Megan set the book back down on the desk, punctuating her words with an emphatic thwack. "Ours isn't a system of hard and fast rules, but of standards."

Outside, voices called out to one another in greeting along the path from Pound to Austin, friends exchanged weekend stories and squirrels made their own little chattering noises, but, inside the Dean's office, all was as chill and quiet as Juliet's crypt.

At long last, the Acting Dean spoke. "An intriguing argument, but in this case, Ms. Milner, the rules *were* quite clear. Even in our antiquated code, any sort of romantic congress between a professor and a student is strictly forbidden."

"Yes, but he's not really a professor, is he? He's not a permanent part of the faculty. He's a lecturer."

"A distinction without a difference, Ms. Milner. For all intents and purposes, he was her professor."

The well-worn phrase, distinction without a difference, threw her back to the comfortable confines of the classroom, to a host of early mornings in Civ Pro or Contracts, fielding question after question, having her arguments ripped to shreds and desperately building them up again, the goal of the game never to give up, never to shrug and admit bewilderment.

Back in the familiar arena of academic argument, Megan felt the thrill of the debate shooting through her veins like a shot of espresso.

"He was her professor, but he retained none of the actual incidents of authority. All the grading rested in my hands. I conducted all the paper conferences and the day to day instruction. The only times during which they interacted in his official capacity was when he gave lecture once a week."

"A podium is a powerful symbol of authority. The psychological pressures cannot be discounted. You remember Chapter Twenty-Five, I presume."

Chapter Twenty-Five, *My Corner Office is Bigger than Yours*, was one of Megan's favorites. The way he had melded Freudian psychology with socio-anthropological studies, and just the lightest dusting of Foucault was nothing short of magisterial.

"No one can deny the validity of Chapter Twenty-Five," Megan said honestly, not noticing as the tight set of Agnelli's lips relaxed. "But in this case, the psychological pressures were outweighed by earlier association. From what I understand, they went to college together and had friends in common."

"You argue," said the Acting Dean, steepling his hands in front of him, "that the fact of their earlier acquaintance ought to outweigh the impropriety."

"I argue," countered Megan, leaning forward with both palms on his desk, "that the fact of their earlier acquaintance cancels out some of the danger of coercive behavior that the rule is expressly constructed to prevent."

"Even if, in this situation, the circumstances were unusual, isn't the principle just as important as the parties? If I allow Mr. Walker to stay on, what's to prevent another lecturer from using this case as precedent? No, Ms. Milner. It can't be done."

"But the law is all about distinguishing between cases, isn't it? Otherwise, we would lose the spirit of the law in our attempts to implement the letter of it."

"Justice, at the expense of the law?"

"Justice, in the interest of the law. If you misapply a law, people lose all respect for it eventually. Think of all the prosecutions for possession of marijuana—or parking violations, for that matter, or any other misdemeanor. The law is better served by judicious application in cases that truly warrant it."

"If you fail to apply a law, Ms. Milner, people conclude—correctly—that they can go on breaking it with impunity. Would you like to see that in the law school?"

Since the only possible answer to that was adverse to her cause, Megan hastily switched rhetorical tacks. "It would be the crassest sort of paternalism to prevent a grown woman from going to a movie with the companion of her choice."

Dean Agnelli regarded her with a jaundiced eye. "Next you'll be speaking to me of the quality of mercy."

Megan countered his gaze unflinchingly. "I'm not asking for mercy, Dean Agnelli. Mercy presupposes a crime by asking for pardon. What I'm asking is for… a more elastic interpretation of the requirements of the code, one in keeping with the purposes for which it was originally intended."

"Elastic rebounds on those who pull it too far."

"I'm not asking you to pull it that far. Please, just consider the alternatives before you make a final decision about Cliff."

"I will… think about it," said the Acting Dean, in the dragging tone of one speaking much against his better judgment.

"You won't regret it," Megan assured him earnestly, leaning forward. "I mean it."

"Why," Agnelli asked very slowly, "might that be?"

"Because," Megan drew herself up to her full height, settling her bag more comfortably on her shoulder, "this can only serve to enhance your reputation as one of our leading scholars on gender issues.

"Ah." A slow change spread across the Acting Dean's face, half-surprised, half-calculating.

Ascribing it to the prospect of academic renown, Megan pressed her advantage. "Just think of the praise you'll get for having found a more nuanced interpretation of sexual harassment guidelines—one that protects women's interests without stripping them of their autonomy. Insulating but not infantilizing," Megan finished triumphantly. "You will have created a whole new paradigm."

"Once paradigms start shifting, it is hard to answer for the consequences."

With an abrupt movement, he rose from the chair, catching at the edge of the desk to steady himself. "Come back tomorrow," he said brusquely. "I'll have my answer for you then."

"Thank you!" Megan's face lit with relief. "I'll see you tomorrow then. Have a good evening!"

And with a little wave, she slipped back again through the glass door, into the sterile second floor hallway.

Dean Agnelli watched as she went, a slim figure in tailored dark pants and a loose black cashmere cardigan. There was nothing about her appearance to call attention to herself. She might have dressed according to his own guidelines on avoiding impropriety in the workplace, neat but not showy, female without being excessively feminine.

And yet….

Despite the mid-day light from the windows, the office suddenly seemed darker, as though clouds had obscured the sun.

Alone in his unaccustomed office, Dean Agnelli sat very still, his eyes fixed unseeing on the space where his visitor had stood. Introspection hung about him, thick as cigar smoke in a Fitzgerald novel.

It was an interesting argument—indefensible, of course, but interesting, nonetheless. The student (Agnelli was quite careful to always use the neutral indicator, even in his own moments of reflection) had revealed a thorough grasp of the intricacies of the subject, even if her analysis had been, in its resolution, flawed. But there had been so much passion in her delivery. Passion for the law, for the pursuits of the mind.

Such intellectual drive ought to be encouraged, rewarded. It was a rare student who cared and thought so deeply, or who spoke so effectively.

That was, of course, why he had agreed to consider her arguments. Nothing more.

And, yet, there might be something to her exposition. Rough around the edges, but something there, nonetheless. Not in its entirety, naturally, but there was a fundamental injustice in preventing two adults, two consenting and equal adults, from consummating their mutual desires.

However, in such cases, the adults were seldom consenting and equal. Cliff Walker would have to be sacrificed. His own authority was too new, the mantle of office hung too uncertainly around his shoulders to admit irregularities.

A point had to made, and the affair had gone too far already. The national media were breathing down his neck and the student groups were up in arms. The women's group had staged a sit-in in protest, the libertarians had staged a counter sit-in in protest of the protest, and the God Squad had already held a candle-lit vigil to pray for the souls of anyone involved, whether they needed it or not. Even the undergrads, cocooned in their playpen, the Yard, had gotten in on the act. The Harvard Crimson had blazed with letters to the editor arguing both for and against sexual congress with the faculty, the rationales ranging from sophisticated expositions of post-modern theory to, "TFs and lecturers are, like, old. And ugly."

The disciplinary committee would meet on Friday morning, and everyone, from the libertarians to the librarians, knew what the outcome would be. He had made no secret of his own sentiments.

Everything militated in favor of continuing on along his original course.

Everything except that patch of empty space in front of his desk and the image of a slim figure in a cashmere cardigan.

"And, then again," murmured the Acting Dean to himself, "why not?"

CHAPTER FOUR

"I have on Angelo imposed the office...
And to behold his sway,
I will, as 'twere a brother of your order,
Visit both prince and people. Therefore, I prithee,
Supply me with the habit and instruct me
How I may formally in person bear
Like a true friar."
  -- I, iii, 40, 43-8

In the center of the living room, Rachel was limbering up in preparation for Yoga for Lawyers (3 credits, M, W, 3:45-5:15).

"What is it today?" asked Megan, as her roommate made a valiant effort to tuck one foot behind her neck and the other around her hip.

"Meditations on the right to privacy and the limits of the courts. This," Rachel was going slightly pop-eyed as she pushed for that final inch, "is *Romer v. Evans*. We're supposed to feel the tension in the law."

Clearly feeling the tension in her tendons, Rachel gave up on *Romer v. Evans* and sank back into *Marbury v. Madison* with visible relief.

"What have you been up to?"

Megan plopped down on the couch, sighing with relief as the weight of her bag slipped off her arm. She massaged her knotted muscles with one hand. "Defending the indefensible."

"I thought that wasn't until next term." Rachel shifted into *Casey v. Planned Parenthood*, one arm stretched protectively across her midriff.

"Not the class. Gabe talked me into speaking into the Dean on behalf of Cliff."

"I thought you liked Cliff."

"I do." Megan relocated her tote bag from couch to floor with unnecessary force. "That's not the point."

Rachel twisted herself upside down for *Roe v. Wade*. "Then what is?"

"What he did goes against everything I stand for. It would be like a vegetarian lobbying for McDonald's."

"They have salads at McDonald's. And yogurt. With granola on top." Rachel's flushed face appeared between her crimson clad legs. One leg read "HARVARD," in descending letters.

"Tell that to the dead cows."

"I don't think cows eat yogurt."

"They don't." Megan left her roommate to her meditations, and wandered into the kitchen. All that talk of yogurt and cows was making her hungry.

In the kitchen, the battered aluminum garbage can was piled high with empty take-away cartons, sure sign that Rachel had gone off her diet over the weekend. The antique sink—installed circa 1922—was completely filled with overturned cups and dirty cutlery. Rachel always meant to do the dishes, but somehow, Megan always did them.

Adding that to her mental To Do list, Megan opened the fridge and peered inside, at a selection consisting of an unopened bag of pre-prepared salad greens gone brown and slimy at the bottom (Rachel's diet phase); a bag of baby carrots (ditto); four bottles of light beer; a carton of skim milk (expiration date yesterday); a container with a half-eaten cheeseburger and pile of rock-hard fries from Cambridge Common, the local burger joint; one lonely cocktail olive, swimming in its briny broth; and two long-expired vanilla yogurts.

Megan took two carrots from the bag. They were slightly slimy around the edges, but they were still orange, so they probably wouldn't kill her. Grocery shopping joined dishwashing on her list, just behind "do Con Law homework," and "break up with Gabe at first opportunity."

One hand still on the open fridge door, she contemplated the cluttered front of the freezer, where printouts of her schedule and Rachel's were tacked one on top of the other, held in place by magnets advertising the virtues of Harvard Health Services, and reminding them to use Lexis Nexis for their research needs. While she was gone over the weekend, someone had started trying to write a message along the bottom of Rachel's schedule with poetry magnets, but had petered out after, "Brief too long; Cannot write; Must drink merry much."

Was that meant to be a haiku? Poetry had never been Megan's thing. And "merry much" made no sense. Frowning slightly, Megan moved the "much" to just after "write," and removed the "merry" altogether. There. That was better.

With the syntax settled to her satisfaction, she checked her schedule. She had Tax at 8:50 tomorrow morning, followed by International Law at 12:40, and Con Law at 4:30, firm interviews at the Charles Hotel at 5:40 and 6:20, and a Journal of Women and the Law editorial meeting at 7:30. Tuesdays were always hellish. She would have to fit in her meeting with Dean Agnelli between her interviews and the editorial board meeting.

A bright yellow post-it stuck to the side of her schedule caught her eye. On it, in Rachel's rounded handwriting, was inscribed, "OCS meeting, Monday 9/26! 3:00, Pound 312."

"Damn!" exclaimed Megan.

"Don't worry!" Rachel's voice floated in from the living room. "I'll do the dishes later!"

"It's not the dishes." Megan slammed the fridge door, and snapped down the last of her baby carrots in two bites. "I forgot about my damn Career Services meeting. It's in—" she contemplated her watch, and cursed again, more vehemently "—five minutes ago. Damn. Stupid Gabe."

"When I went Friday," said Rachel reassuringly, her voice only slightly muffled from hanging upside down, "they were running half an hour late."

"I hope they still are," said Megan sourly, trying to wriggle into her shoes and grab for her bag at the same time. "If Gabe's made me miss my OCS meeting, I will *murder* him."

"There's a new guy at OCS. Kind of dorky, but he gave me some really good advice."

"Dorky?" Megan flung her seventy pound Con Law book out of her bag like a ship's captain jettisoning cargo.

"Seventies hair," explained Rachel with a shudder, while Megan's tax book joined her Con Law book on the floor. "I could feel my hair starting to frizz just looking at it. He suggested I look into going in-house somewhere. Like a tv studio, or a magazine company."

"But you don't know anything about entertainment law."

"When has that ever been a prerequisite for getting a job? Besides," said Rachel self-righteously, "I read Entertainment Weekly."

"Those things are filled with outmoded stereotypes." Megan conducted a final bag check. Blackberry, cell phone, computer, interview schedule, resume, curriculum vitae, hair brush. All present and accounted for.

"Oh, I just get them for the pictures. Aren't you going to be late?"

"Going!" called Megan, and slammed the door behind her.

She would have taken the shortest way to campus if there were one, but Cambridge had been devised along a plan similar to that of a carnival funhouse. Lines that seemed straight tilted off to an angle, taking the unwary pedestrian blocks out of the way; streets circled around for no apparent reason, and wherever one wanted to go, there was sure to be a building in the way. Charging down the rutted pavement of Oxford Street, she took a sharp right just after the grad school dorms, past a glass sliver of a building dedicated to the pursuit of technological incomprehensibilities, across a quad that looked like it ought to belong to the Law School, but mostly didn't.

Even though the weather was mild, she felt uncomfortably overheated by the time she darted across the plaza fronting Harkness, towards the dark overhang of Pound Hall, grim even in the middle of the day. Under her cashmere cardigan, her white tank-top clung clammily to her skin.

The unseasonably pleasant weather had brought out the student body from their usual holes in the classrooms and tunnels. They were all clustered around the piazza, sitting at the little metal tables and loitering in groups along the walkway. In homage to the fact that the weather had gone above sixty-five degrees, most of the women were in tank tops, many in flip-flops and floaty summer skirts, others in jeans that hugged their calves and trailed well below their fashionably flat shoes. Some guys, heeding the universal call of the sun, had removed their shirts and were engaged in flinging a Frisbee just off the edge of the paved area.

What was it about good weather that induced men to remove clothing for no particular reason? And why did they always have to fling projectiles at one another while they did it? Megan ducked and increased her pace as the Frisbee, flying low, narrowly missed her arm. They were no better than apes, jumping up and down and showing off their muscles to impress the female of the species. The females of the species, unfortunately, were showing every sign of appreciation, as evidenced by a wad of dramatically flipped hair that nearly dislodged one of Meghan's contact lenses.

Megan impartially resented them all at the moment. Between Gabe, Cliff, and the increasingly worrisome memory of her conversation with the Acting Dean, she had no patience for the Mating Dance of the Amorous Law Student, especially when it involved making her even later for her Office of Career Services appointment than she already was. Hiking her bag more firmly onto her shoulder, she elbowed her way through the loafing louts with a series of pointed, "Ex*cuse* me… *if* you don't mind… *thank* you!"

Her phone started shrilling just as she slammed through the heavy glass door into the relative peace of Pound Hall.

Striding past a wall covered with black and white pictures of faculty members, some almost unrecognizable in their youthful guises, she dug into her bag for her phone. Professor Agnelli's picture was there, with a pointed seventies collar, and hair that hadn't yet gone gray around the edges, next to a picture of a female professor Megan didn't know, with granny glasses and stick-straight hair held back by a folded bandana.

Megan flipped her phone open without checking to see who it was. "Yes?"

"How did it go?"

Gabe. She should have known. If he were around, he would probably be shirtless and throwing something.

The reflection did nothing to improve her temper.

"I don't know," Megan said tersely, speed-walking past the coffee urns towards the staircase. By three o'clock, unfortunately, the coffee urns were already empty, even if she had to time to stop at them, which she didn't, all thanks to Gabe. "I'm supposed to see Dean Agnelli again tomorrow."

"Not a no…. Hey, that's pretty good."

Megan's teeth gritted in a way that boded ill for thirteen-plus years of expensive orthodontal work. "Break up with Gabe" moved precipitately up from #9 on the To Do List (just behind "grocery shopping" and "do dishes") to #1. In bold.

"Gabe, we need to find a time to talk. Soon."

In the basement of Gannet House, Gabe turned over another card in his current round of Party Poker. "I always want to talk to you, beautiful."

"That's not what I mean."

"Shit! The copier just exploded. Gotta go." With expert timing, Gabe hit the red off button just before Megan could start spluttering.

"God, I'm good," he said, flinging the phone down on the floor next to his chair, where it landed with a slight crackle on top of an empty bag of barbecue-flavored potato chips.

"Are you going to let her break up with you?" Dan kicked back in his battered easy chair, reaching for another beer.

"Nah." Gabe pushed a button, flipping a card onto the discard pile. "Not until this Cliff business is cleared up, anyway. Besides, she's kind of cute when she's all worked up."

Back in the third floor of Pound Hall, Megan slammed the phone shut, wasting precious time glowering at the worthless hunk of metal. "Jerk."

"Man trouble?" asked the woman at the desk sympathetically, pushing her long, gray braid back over the shoulder of her flowered caftan. Her nameplate read Rainbow Dawn Summers.

Megan wondered whether it was a requirement of OCS that its employees dress like refugees from Woodstock, or whether like simply called to like.

Megan stuffed the phone into her bag, chalking up another black mark against Gabe. "I don't think he qualifies."

"None of them do, sweetie, none of them do." The gray braid, tied with a bit of the same yarn that protruded from her knitting bag, shook sadly. Megan half-expected a chorus of R-E-S-P-E-C-T to follow, but Rainbow Dawn settled for a more conventional, "How can I help you?"

"I have—had—a 3:00 appointment with…" Megan consulted her blackberry. "Mr. Friar."

"He's still with his 2:40," said Rainbow Dawn. "Why don't you just take a seat, and look through the Vault Guides, and I'm sure he'll be with you in a moment."

"Thank you," said Megan, and took a seat as directed at the unwieldy pine table in the center of the room. The table had been ingeniously constructed of four smaller tables jammed together, creating a whole just large enough that the dog-eared binders and Vault Guides in the middle were completely unreachable from any point around the sides.

As drab as every other room in Pound Hall, the Office of Career Services looked like a cross between a lower school classroom and a doctor's waiting room. It was decorated in shades of beige, its pitted plasterboard walls covered with curling flyers advertising various seminars and job opportunities, some of them long since past. Along two of the whisper-thin walls, doors advertised the presence of interior offices, tiny cubbyholes of space where the staff of OCS counseled and cajoled the student body into their future employment. Megan could hear the staccato rhythm of agitated voices from all six offices; it was the height of interview season and everyone was getting panicky. "But I *want* to work at an IP firm," floated from one, while from another simply came the sound of dismal sobbing.

A door opened behind Megan, and a demoralized-looking boy, his baseball cap pulled low over his forehead, slunk out, followed by a man in brown corduroy pants, a white oxford shirt, and a diamond-patterned sweater vest in shades of blue and yellow. He consulted a clipboard in his hand. "Ms... Milner?" he said.

"Hi." Megan raised an unenthusiastic hand and maneuvered herself and her bag out of the chair, which had been constructed neither for aesthetics nor convenience. "I'm Megan. Nice to meet you."

Megan could see what Rachel had meant by dorky. Mr. Friar's black hair looked as though it had been washed in salt water and styled with an egg-beater. It stood out from his face in corkscrews reminiscent of such entertainment luminaries as Ronald McDonald and Bozo the Clown. He even had the mustache to go with it, a droopy thing that made Megan think of late night episodes of "All in the Family," plaid bell-bottoms, and her mother's old collection of Sonny and Cher records.

In keeping with his hairstyle, Mr. Friar's glasses were large and square, framed in thick brown plastic, spanning his face from well above his brows to the very base of his nose. The style had looked quite glamorous on Audrey Hepburn, but was somewhat less so thirty years later, in the arid confines of an OCS office.

"Bob Friar." For an OCS employee, Mr. Friar's handshake was surprisingly firm, and not at all clammy. "Sorry to keep you waiting," he added, gesturing her into his cubbyhole ahead of him. "Some resumes need more work than others."

Which, Megan thought smugly, would not be hers.

Megan didn't have to ask which chair to take, since there were only two in the room, and one had a jacket draped over it, brown herringbone with tweed patches on the sleeves. Megan seated herself in the other, pulling up her knees as far as possible to give Mr. Friar room to pass. She could tell he was new, because the cube lacked the usual indicia of occupancy; there were no cheerful photos of children, wife, or dog in brightly painted ceramic frames, no novelty mugs, and no masterpieces of high finger-painting. Instead, the tiny office, with its built in counter that ran around two walls and served as both desk and storage space, was overwhelmed with brightly colored folders, spilling forth resumes and transcripts. The only personal touch was a straggling row of books on one of the crooked shelves bolted into the wall. A Complete Shakespeare, the poems of Yeats, and a smattering of books by an author named Evelyn Waugh—a woman, Megan supposed, although she had never heard of her—gave some indication of how OCS's new hire spent his leisure hours.

"Has it been busy?" Megan asked, just to be polite, as Mr. Friar squeezed past her, and folded himself into his desk chair. Like everything else about the office, the chair was too small for his frame; Megan wouldn't have placed any bets on its—or his—lasting out the year.

"I had no idea it could be this busy," he said sincerely, accepting the folder she handed him, and leafing through the contents. "Resume... transcript... excellent."

As he leaned forward to examine her resume, his hair slipped slightly. Poor man, he must be balding and not have come to terms with it. It was really rather sad, between the toupee and the tiny office.

"You have your on campus interviews scheduled?" he asked, looking up. His hair might have been slipping, but the eyes behind the dirty spectacles were good-humored, and not the least bit pathetic.

"Yes." Megan efficiently handed over another piece of paper, with a printed list of fifteen on campus interview appointments scattered over the next two weeks. "I have Kynder, Jentler at 5:40 tomorrow, and Pharse & Maquerie at 6:10, both in the Charles."

"Pharse & Maquerie? Their reputation with female associates is poor, to say the least."

"That's exactly why I put them on the list."

"You plan to infiltrate from within? It's a noble goal, but it might make life personally awkward for you."

"Without a little personal discomfort, the civil rights movement would never have happened. Or women's suffrage."

"Well, I don't think they're going to handcuff you to a fire hydrant, so there's that, at least. They might handcuff you to your desk, but that's pretty standard across the board."

"Oh, I'm not afraid of hard work," said Megan quickly.

"I can see that from your resume. Battered women's shelter, Board of Student Advisors, *Journal of Women and the Law*, Legal Aid, Living Wage Committee, *Review for Social Justice and International Equality*... you might want to move this over so all your journals are together." He turned the resume so she could see it, indicating with the tip of his pen. It was a surprisingly nice pen, silver, with a gold nib. But, then, Mr. Friar clearly didn't spend his money on his wardrobe. "It makes it easier for the reader if you arrange your activities thematically, rather than alphabetically."

Megan made a note. "I'll remember that for the future."

Mr. Friar hesitated over her resume for a moment. Megan leaned forward and tried to read over his shoulder, to see what was causing such perturbation. Had she misspelled something? Forgotten to italicize *summa cum laude*, or left a p out of *phi beta kappa*?

"I can't help but notice that you TF-ed for Cliff Walker," he finally said.

"Yes. You don't think that will prejudice my employment opportunities, do you?"

Mr. Friar looked up in surprise, his hair tipping precipitously. He hastily righted it. "No! No, nothing of the kind. Many of these partners don't read anything other than the American Lawyer—and even if they do, they probably won't put two and two together. I was simply curious."

"You're not the only one," said Megan, thinking of Rachel's complaints about the constant phoning of news networks over the weekend.

"If you'll forgive my asking, what do you think of him?"

"I have a great deal of respect for him as a scholar," said Megan primly.

"But you disapprove," supplied Mr. Friar, smiling so understandingly that Megan felt her tense shoulders begin to relax.

"Strongly," admitted Megan. "I just don't understand what he was thinking. He had to know it was against the rules."

"Maybe he thought they wouldn't be enforced." The mustache twisted wryly. "I understand they hadn't been in a while."

"Even so," said Megan, rearranging herself in her chair, "you can't just break rules because you think they won't be enforced."

"But we do," said Mr. Friar, "all the time. Think about all the times you've jaywalked, or music you may have downloaded, or even the times you've parked somewhere without a permit in the expectation you wouldn't get caught. We all do it."

"But those—" Megan caught herself before she could fall into his trap. There were a hundred ways she could try to justify jaywalking—as a silly law, as a victimless crime, and so on—but every single one of those justifications could be turned right back against her.

"It's different," she said, and felt like a two year old for it.

Mr. Friar looked at her kindly, as if he understood her irritation. "Do you think Cliff Walker should be asked to leave?"

"I spoke to Dean Agnelli about that this morning."

"To ask him to fire him?"

Megan shook her head, so slightly that her hair barely trembled with the movement. "No," she said. "To ask him to let Cliff stay."

"Did you?" Mr. Friar's wig listed to the side.

"Mm-hmm," Megan nodded ruefully, feeling slightly sick at the memory of the conversation. "He asked me to come back tomorrow. He said he wanted time to think it over."

"You must have made quite an impression on him."

"Not a good one."

"I wouldn't say that. Arthur wouldn't ask you back if he didn't really intend to think it over. He doesn't play those sorts of games."

"Arthur?"

"We've known each other for dog's years. But it's a long story and you have interviews to get through tomorrow."

Megan recognized a dismissal when she heard one. Retrieving her resume, she tucked it back away in her bag. "Thank you for all your help."

"Think nothing of it." Mr. Friar rose, pressing back against the bookshelves to allow her room to pass. His exuberant hair made Evelyn Waugh's *Vile Bodies* totter on its precarious perch at the end of the shelf. "And, about Arthur—"

Megan looked back over her shoulder. Mr. Friar paused in the doorway, leaning one hand against the jamb, and looked intently at her. Through the dirty lenses of his glasses, it was impossible to tell what color his eyes were. Megan wondered how he managed to see out of them—and how well he knew Dean Agnelli.

"Yes?"

"I wouldn't worry about making a bad impression if I were you. Whatever you said, it must have been pretty powerful stuff."

"I tried," said Megan simply, hitching her bag back up over her shoulder.

Mr. Friar smiled. "If you have time, come back and let me know how it goes."

"I will," said Megan, and was surprised to find she meant it.

CHAPTER FIVE

"Ignominy in ransom and free pardon
Are of two houses; lawful mercy
Is nothing kin to foul redemption."
    -- II, iv, 111-114

A clutch of law students crammed like crows into the elevator of the Charles Hotel. Each wore a black suit, pants for the men, skirts for the girls. The boys wore carefully calibrated blue or red ties, the girls a simple strand of pearls. Each clutched an identical, leather-bound portfolio. The contents of the portfolio were, almost without exception, the same. A resume, printed on thick, cream colored paper. A transcript, duly issued from the registrar's office, in bright shades of crimson for those who were proud of their first year's results and wanted to showcase them as they deserved, or a cheap printout, slightly askew on grainy copier paper, for those who preferred their transcript slightly smeared, in the hopes the happy confluence of a minus and a dust mote might produce an unintentional elevation in score.

All around Megan, fragments of conversation swirled and subsided, punctuated by nervous laughter, the shuffle of black-shod feet against the elevator carpet, and the moist munching of chocolate-covered pretzels purloined from the firms' hospitality suites.

"Wouldn't work anywhere but New York, of course—" said a girl to Megan's right, her suit too tight across her chest.

"—bastard of an interviewer—" came from another corner, a boy so tall that his suit pants looked like he had been caught in the middle of a tug of war in Brooks Brothers.

"As my father, the judge, always says—I did mention that my father is a judge, right?"

"And then he, like, pointed to the bed, and I was, like—"

The elevator pinged in warning before the doors opened on eight, disgorging Megan, in her black suit, with her leather portfolio under one arm. The door slid smoothly shut before she could tell whether the girl in the back had been recapping her weekend, or her interview. It might have been either.

Megan made a mental note to bring up the impropriety of holding interviews in hotel rooms at that night's editorial board meeting for the Journal of Women and the Law. Someone ought to write an editorial deploring the practice. Men were simple creatures; they couldn't help but get ideas. Even if the interviewer were circumspect about keeping to the table, the bed was still there, exuding its symbolic power, just as Professor Agnelli discussed in Chapter Twenty-Five of *Legal Bodies*.

The thought of *Legal Bodies* sent Megan's taut nerves reverberating like a wind harp.

How had she let Gabe railroad her into yesterday's fiasco? Just remembering made her feel as though she were being rolled slowly through a field of ground glass; every recollection stung, worse than the blisters from her unaccustomed pumps.

By rote, Megan followed the signs towards Pharse & Maquerie's hospitality suite. A right, a right, and another right again, down a bland hotel corridor dotted with doors. Dean Agnelli had graciously agreed to receive her that evening to discuss Cliff's fate. He had, he said in his email, taken some time to think over her intriguing ideas and had gathered some thoughts to share with her on the topic.

Which, Megan knew all too well, was scholar-speak for "your argument sucked, but at least you tried." Wince-worthy enough when one was having a paper reviewed, but even worse when one's career hung in the balance. It took Megan a moment to remember that it was supposed to be Cliff's career, not hers that was at issue.

Well, it was her career, too. Agnelli bestrode women's legal studies like a colossus. In his hands lay the power to confer or withhold recommendation letters, reviews, grants, the full panoply of the scholar's arsenal. A pat on the right back, and she might find herself a Fellow at a prestigious institute; an elegantly worded damnation of praise, the sort that began "Megan is a very conscientious student," and she would be doomed to a career as a corporate lawyer, throwing sops to her conscience by chairing the in-house

Women's Committee, where former feminists arranged boat cruises and cocktail receptions for prospective female associates while their male colleagues merrily went on occupying the corner offices and trading privileged information in the sanctum of the urinal.

Ahead of her, a boldly lettered sign propped on a wooden easel announced that she had achieved the Pharse & Maquerie hospitality suite, "Pharse & Maquerie: Celebrating 125 years of Legal Excellence." Exactly whose legal excellence they were celebrating was left deliberately unclear; as far as Megan knew, the firm had only been founded just before World War I, even if the firm literature did claim a lineage that went back to negotiating the original charter for Plymouth Plantation.

Through the open door, Megan could see a legal anthill of dark suits in the navy and pine confines of the hotel suite. Along one wall, the hotel had made a half-hearted nod to refreshment: three urns on a stained white cloth, reading "Coffee," "Decaf," and "Hot Water," surrounded by the usual debris of torn tea bags and damp sugar packets. They were accompanied by the sort of thick white mug designed to drip on the unfortunate drinker, and a selection of comestibles chiefly notable for their crumb-shedding capacities. All through the suite, students surreptitiously swiped at pretzel crumbs, wincing as chocolate smeared brown on white shirt cuffs.

It was the opening test. Could one eat a chocolate pretzel with dignity? Megan wondered if there was a section for that on the interviewers' forms, with checkboxes for a) crumbs on jacket, b) chocolate on teeth, c) conspicuous coffee stains.

Megan scrupulously avoided the refreshments.

Across from the refreshment table, firm literature had been fanned out in an attractive arc, a series of booklets all bound in the firm's signature maroon, a shade darker than Harvard crimson, but still unmistakably of the same family. Gold lettering engraved deeply into the covers read, "A Brief History of the Firm," "A Day in the Life of a Pharse Associate," and, like a somewhat anemic family album, "Our 2005 Summer Associates." Megan wouldn't have been surprised to open it to find sepia photos of Baby's First Brief, appropriately edged in gold-tinged triangles. Instead, the glossy pages contained carefully cropped headshots, two per page, each accompanied by the individual's academic pedigree: undergraduate and graduate institutions, degree, and year of graduation, like a stud book for the academically inclined.

Megan shifted automatically out of the way as someone brushed by her, glancing up from her perusal of Yale-Harvard, Harvard-Yale, enlivened by the occasional Princeton-Penn. Megan felt sorry for the lone Cornell grad.

"Meg!" Someone grabbed her in a back-thumping embrace, but it was the wrong someone. Megan's nose was mashed into pinstriped wool, none too fresh after a full week of interviews. "Hey."

"Hey, yourself," said Megan sourly. Paul was not high on her list of favorite people under any circumstances; recent events had demoted him to somewhere just above the orthodontist and beneath the clerk at the post office. "Do you have an interview?"

Paul nodded. "Six-ten." He gazed worshipfully around the room, his watery blue eyes taking in the glossy pictures of smiling associates, the P&M logo draped across one wall, the blackberries clipped nonchalantly to hip or hand as associates mingled casually with their future colleagues. "I've always wanted to work at a place like Pharse."

So, Megan had no doubt, did Gabe. It was just his sort of place, an old boys' club by another name, famed for having the worst female retention rate in the city. Her decision to interview had been more a matter of thumbing her nose than a genuine career option.

If the meeting with Agnelli went as poorly as prophesied, she might have to start taking it more seriously.

Paul tugged at her elbow. "Have you spoken to the Dean again?"

"Not yet."

"We'd really appreciate…." Paul began.

"We?" Megan interrupted. "Who is this we, all of a sudden? And why do you all care so damn much about—"

"We all care at Pharse & Maquerie!" said a voice brightly behind them.

A woman with sleek blonde hair pulled back into a French braid bore down upon them, cradling a clipboard loaded with a pile of maroon brochures in her left arm. Her suit was as dark as anyone else's, but rather than a crisp blouse and pearls, she wore a silk knit top and too much chunky gold jewelry, the ultimate identifier of Legal Personnel.

Drawing himself up out of his usual slump, Paul thrust out a hand, in a shake clearly calibrated to combine assertiveness and deference. Not too much deference, though, since she was only recruiting personnel, after all. "Hi. I'm Paul Hines."

"Tina Slattery. And you are…?" She squinted at Megan with phony goodwill, like a doctor's receptionist. Her eyes were brown, like the roots of her hair.

"Megan Milner. I have a six-ten."

"Well, you're just on time, then." Instead of gold stars, she doled out maroon brochures, three for each of them. "This is our firm history—as you'll see, we have a long history of promoting legal excellence. Only the best of the best at Pharse!"

"Didn't Maquerie personally defend the Board in *Brown v. Board*?" asked Megan.

"We're involved in many high profile cases," said Tina importantly, rustling through brochures. Brown was not a color that interested her. "That's just one of the many benefits of working at Pharse. As you can see in 'A Day in the Life of a Pharse Associate,' unlike other firms, we give you real responsibility right away. You get real work for real clients."

"That's just what I want," averred Paul, the man most noted among Megan's 1L section for his ability to remain supine for days on end. "Real work."

Tina beamed appreciatively. "At Pharse, we're a team. We take people from all walks of life"—as long, Megan noticed, as those walks happened to be the better Ivy League law schools—"and turn them into Pharsicals. That's our little name for our junior associates," she confided.

Paul's piggy eyes took on a faraway expression as he imagined himself a Pharsical. He would undoubtedly have worn a beanie, too, if the job description had called for it.

"We don't discriminate on grounds of race, religion, gender, sexual orientation, or even physical handicap." Tina's gold rings created their own light as she gestured towards a man sitting in a wheelchair in the corner of the room, pounding text into his blackberry with decisive thrusts of the finger. "Over there you can see Tim, our disabled lawyer."

Tim waved a crutch in greeting.

"Tim has overcome all sorts of hardships to be where he is. Of course, we did have to make sure his office was on an elevator-accessible floor. But at Pharse, we're willing to make those sorts of sacrifices in pursuit of excellence."

Paul looked suitably impressed at the delicacy of mind that would disturb office allocation for wheelchair access.

"If you'll just look through our list of last year's summer associates"—Tina rustled rapidly through the maroon-covered brochure, sending faces leaping sideways like a reel in an old black and white film—"you'll see we value diversity highly at Pharse. Only last year, we had a summer from Montana!"

Who had matriculated at Yale Law, and done his undergrad at Harvard. There couldn't be much Montana left in the man.

Peering over Tina's shoulder, Megan was quite impressed by the sameness of it all. In the pictures of the women, pearls gleamed and hair was almost universally glossy. One imagined that the two frizzy haired exceptions wouldn't last terribly long. As for the men, it was amazing how wide a collection of junior jowls one could find among the law school population. They had already begun to sport the signs of legal prominence—prominent forehead (accentuated by receding hairlines), bulbous eyes, and bulging jowls. All indicia of either intense mental effort or a tie pulled too tight.

"What about pro bono?" asked Megan.

"The firm is deeply committed to pro bono work," recited Tina. "If you look at our 'A Day in the Life' brochure, you'll see that there are many pro bono opportunities to choose among. Pharse lawyers have worked with the Squirrel Defense League—we wrote an amicus brief strongly advocating the poisoning of pigeons in the Park—the Home for Retired Partners, the Hamptons Protection Commission…. Why, we logged as many as sixty pro bono hours last year!"

"Per lawyer?"

"Um, no. As a firm."

Paul looked relieved.

"It's nearly 6:08! I'd feel awful if I made you late for your interviews, and I know you'll want a moment to pull yourself together before you go in. Let's see…."

Consulting her clipboard, Tina ran one pink-lacquered finger down a closely typed spreadsheet. The shade of the nail polish was carefully calibrated not to clash with the Pharse brochures.

"Paul, you'll be meeting with Ron Amberson in room 815. He's a partner in Corporate, and I think you'll have a very good time with him. And, Megan, we have you down for one of our litigation partners, Ken Rolfe, in 804. He spearheaded that pro bono pigeon brief, so you two should have a lot to talk about. Good luck, you two!"

All around the room, a similar shooing process was going on. Like a school of fish, the dark suited wave flowed across the room, leaving bits of maroon detritus in its wake.

Megan only had time to murmur to Paul, "Tell Gabe I need to speak to him. Like, *now*," before someone brushed between them, making determinedly for the door and future legal excellence on the Pharse & Maquerie model.

In the hallway, like cadets in a military review, students took their places at evenly spaced intervals in front of the hotel room doors, skirt seams aligned, ties tightened, portfolios held firmly (exhibiting confidence), but not too firmly (a damning admission of fear) beneath rapidly dampening armpits. No matter how much deodorant had been slapped on, a combination of fear and artificial fibers combined to combat it, filling the hallway with the sour grapefruit smell of sweat. Or, rather, perspiration. An aspiring Pharsical would never stoop to anything so plebian as sweat; that was Legal Aid attorneys, who earned a mere $80,000 a year and never got to fly first class.

In front of 804, Megan shook her cuff back and consulted her watch, setting off a ripple effect of cuff-shaking and watch-checking all down the hall. The door inched open, and a pudgy girl squeezed her suited form through the frame.

"He said to tell you he'll be right with you."

"Thanks." Through the closed door, Megan could hear water running.

When Megan ventured into the hotel room, her interviewer was already seated at the table that passed as a desk.

He didn't stand as she entered. He didn't even bother to look up. Instead, he continued to scrutinize the paper in front of him. As she crossed the room, Megan recognized it as a copy of the resume she had submitted through the electronic on campus recruiting system. The paper must have been set crookedly in the printer; all of Megan's carefully hoarded accomplishment listed to the left on a drunken diagonal. Her summer experience doing pro bono work at The Haven, a home for battered women, had disappeared right off the side of the page.

Mr. Rolfe didn't waste time with amenities like introductions. He cut right to the chase, in a manner that must have disarmed many a hapless junior associate, and perhaps even the odd opposing counsel.

"You're not on Law Review."

"No." Megan carefully pulled out the chair on the other side of tiny metal table and inserted herself into it. "I believed the interests of the community would be better served by putting my talents to work at a publication with fewer resources at its disposal."

Mr. Rolfe translated that. "You mean you didn't get on."

"I mean I never applied. My interests didn't lie in that direction."

Rolfe grunted, and returned to her resume. He had been on Law Review, and therefore everyone must want to be on Law Review. It was an immutable law of nature, sure as the fixed planets in their spheres and the advent of the Superbowl on a set Sunday.

He ran the back of his pen dismissively down the list of carefully accumulated activities: the journals, the shelters, the activist organizations. Easing her transcript out of its leather casing, Megan nudged it across the table towards him. Mr. Rolfe ignored it.

"Looking at your resume, Miss Milner, only one word comes to mind. Lame. What do you have to say to that?"

Megan folded her hands neatly in her lap, and regarded the hairs bristling from his nose. A large liver spot crept along the side of his nose, like a toadstool.

"Listening to your comment, only one word comes to mind. Rude. What do you have to say to that?"

"I'd say that you—" looking down, Mr. Rolfe found her grades looking right back up at him, a clear sweep of A's and A-'s emblazoned in crimson, like a royal flush. "—have spunk. And we like spunk at Pharse & Maquerie."

Which, Megan knew very well, translated to "we like your grade point average."

Mr. Rolfe shifted back in his chair, propping one leg against the opposite knee, exuding cozy bonhomie like old scotch. "Is there anything I can tell you about the firm? Anything you would like to know?"

Megan slid her cuff back from her watch under the table. If she left now and really booked it back to campus, she might manage to skid in on the outer edge of on-time. She was sure that OCS had some sort of rule about not leaving an on-campus interview after only ten minutes ("because if you don't respect the firm, they won't respect you"), but she just didn't care. She didn't respect the firm. And she didn't care whether or not they respected her.

"I really can't think of anything," said Megan, pushing back her chair. "Thank you for your time."

"I could put you in touch with one of our female associates if you'd prefer—get the rundown from someone younger, eh?"

"No," said Megan. "I believe I've heard quite enough."

Blissfully impervious to any insult he hadn't delivered, Mr. Rolfe inserted her resume and transcript deftly into the right side of his own portfolio, maroon and embossed with the Pharse logo, a golden goose brooding in a nest of briefs. There were very few resumes on the right side, Megan noticed, and those that were were all the thick cream and crimson of the graded aristocracy. On the left, a sheaf of photocopies bristled like a ledger of lost hopes.

Rising, Rolfe held out a hand. It was plump, and slightly clammy, with a wide gold wedding band indenting the third finger of his left hand. "The Pharse reputation does speak for itself. Why waste time, eh?"

"I couldn't agree more," said Megan. She only wished she hadn't wasted the time on the interview.

Across the length of the Yard, past the freshman houses and the Science Center, away in the upper reaches of Griswold Hall, Mrs. Dexter had gone home, but the Acting Dean was still there. He sat at his desk at the far end of the room, his craggy head bowed over a pile of papers. Autumn dusk had fallen over the office, but the Acting Dean hadn't turned on the lights. He read by the beam of a small desk lamp that illuminated the immediate area like the spotlight in a Broadway show just before a sad, slow song.

His pen flicked out, then withdrew, annotating, underscoring, correcting.

He raised his head as Megan took a tentative step into the room, her pumps clicking lightly against the uncarpeted floor. The Persian carpet had gone the way of the old Dean, taking with it any hope of camouflage.

"I'm so sorry to be late," said Megan hurriedly. "I had an interview that ran over…."

"It is that season, isn't it?" said the Acting Dean, with the detached air of one who looks on tempests, but, having never departed the shelter of the academy, is not shaken. "With whom?"

"Pharse & Maquerie," admitted Megan.

Agnelli retracted the point of his pen with a neat click. It was plastic, with the logo of a hotel chain down one side. "Pharse? A surprising choice for one of your background."

"I saw it as infiltrating the enemy." Megan shifted her weight off one blistered heel onto the other. "After all, as you pointed out in *Legal Bodies*, nothing is ever going to change as long as the actors themselves are complicit with the system."

"Ah, but you forgot the message of Chapter Twenty-Three."

"That Long, Good Night?" That chapter, as Megan remembered, had been quite clear. Those who went into the system intending to change it wound up being seduced by the perks of the job. Taking cars home on the client, drinking on the firm's tab, charging fresh underwear to Office General (the all-purpose firm account), they were too busy to dwell on ideological issues and too cosseted to complain. After a year, what had once seemed objectionable had become normal.

"I should have paid more attention to that," said Megan ruefully. "I just assumed it couldn't be me."

"As so many do." Clearly, she had exonerated herself, since Agnelli laid down his pen in the center of his blotter, and regarded Megan directly from under the shock of rough hair at his brow. "I doubt you would go gently."

"Thank you." Under the panacea of praise, even her blisters seemed to sting less. "That's very kind of you."

"Honest," said Agnelli, somehow contriving to look craggier than ever. "Not kind."

"About Cliff…." Megan began hesitantly.

"Ah. The unfortunate Mr. Walker." Agnelli forestalled her with one raised hand. "You should be aware that the final decision does not rest in my hands."

Megan could feel her smile curdling. "Of course. I understand." That was professor-speak for "No can do," just as "Your paper was very interesting," stood for, "Hey, at least you tried."

"However," Agnelli paused, regarding her thoughtfully, as though weighing whether to go on, "I do have a certain modicum of influence with the committee. My background in these matters...."

He let the impact of those ellipses seep into the air between them, infusing it like the bouquet of a heavy port.

Megan waded into the mist of the unspoken meanings. "Would you be willing to speak for Cliff?"

"That," said Agnelli, "depends."

"I am sure that Cliff would be ready to meet any condition you might set. He's learned his lesson."

"It's not Cliff I was thinking of." Megan's mind drifted from student protests to alumni pressure, sketching together the outlines of arguments, as Agnelli watched her thoughtfully. Abruptly, he said, "You do agree, don't you, that the only defensible ideology is a lived one?"

"Yes, but...." Mentally drafting a letter to the alumni, Megan was taken off guard.

"It's all in the interpretation of the living of it?" Agnelli filled in for her. "No, Ms. Milner. You can do better than that."

"I don't understand what you mean."

"You argue that the rules ought not to apply where there are two consenting adults—although we could quibble about the definitions of those two terms—and the power relationship is so attenuated as to produce no threat of actual coercion. Does that summarize your position?"

"Yes." Megan drew out the word, searching for the booby-trap beneath the verbiage. "Essentially. If the rules are designed to prohibit the use of academic threats to secure personal favors then they can't be meant to apply where there isn't that coercive element."

"And you stand by that argument?"

Megan nodded.

"In that case, give the proof of it by living it."

Megan frowned in confusion. "Aren't I doing that, by speaking up for Cliff?"

"Advocacy and internalization are two very different things. If you really believe that what Cliff and Julia did is blameless, be the proof of it."

Agnelli leaned back in his chair, the lamplight ringing the graying hair above his brow with a crown of fire.

"Come to dinner with me."

CHAPTER SIX

"Isabella: *I know your virtue hath a license in't,*
Which seems a little fouler than it is,
To pluck on others.

Angelo: *Believe me, on mine honor,*
My words express my purpose."
      -- II, iv, 145-148.

"To whom should I complain? Did I tell this
Who would believe me? O perilous mouths,
That bear in them one and the selfsame tongue,
Either of condemnation or aproof,
Bidding the law make curtsy to their will."
      -- II, iv, 171-175

"This is a sort of test, isn't it? A hypothetical!" The answer was so obvious that Megan couldn't believe she hadn't spotted it before. "If I say no, you point out that I've just condemned my own argument on behalf of Cliff. But the cases are distinguishable. In Cliff and Julia's case, Cliff's power over Julia was attenuated by the presence of an intermediary—me—who exercised actual power. In this case—"

Agnelli regarded her indulgently, almost avuncularly. "This is not a hypothetical, Ms. Milner."

Megan pressed her lips very tightly together. "Then what is it?"

"Consider it an invitation."

"An invitation," Megan repeated numbly.

Agnelli remained where he was, seated behind the desk. "An invitation to closer acquaintance," he said, as casually as if he were giving her a research assignment. "I believe we have much to offer one another."

"And if the answer were to be no?"

"Why, then you would have no opportunity to persuade me of the merits of Mr. Walker's case."

"I could write you a memo."

"Such persuasion is best done in person."

"I express myself better in writing."

Agnelli leaned back in his chair, out of the halo of the desk lamp. "Some projects, however, require a collaborative effort. A discourse. A give and take. Can I make myself any clearer—Megan?"

There was only one thing she could possibly do. "I think I should leave now."

"Evading the issue?" Agnelli shook his head, his shadow shaking with him in the aureole of the desk lamp. "I hadn't thought you would bend so easily."

Was he testing her commitment to her theory? Perhaps she was meant to prove her feminist bona fides by riding straight into the canon's mouth like a one woman Light Brigade. Only if she showed the strength of will to resist an advance herself would she be worthy to condone Cliff—or something like that. It didn't follow logically, but then, nothing had gone logically since Megan had entered the shadowed office.

"I could report you," she said tentatively, watching Agnelli closely. "I could tell everyone that you demanded personal favors in exchange for professional guidance."

"You could. But who would believe you? You have," Agnelli said gently, "no evidence. Unless you brought a recording device with you?"

Megan shook her head mutely.

"I thought not. Even if you had, everyone would assume it was a forgery. My reputation is too well established. You are merely a student. Students are notoriously prone to fits of hysteria. Whereas I...." Agnelli spread his hands wide in a self-deprecating gesture more effective than the loudest boasts.

His past projects scrolled through the air between them, like an enchanter's illusion. From the walls, Megan could feel the pictures pressing down on her, all advocates for the opposition. "Arthur? Sexual harassment?" they seemed to say. "Why it was more likely the other way around! Poor girl... must have had a crush... clearly unhinged...." Agnelli would gaze benignly down upon it all like the Lincoln monument, weathered but unbroken.

Meanwhile, she would be labeled a loony, as surely as any Victorian heroine shuffled off to an asylum by a complaisant family doctor.

Megan writhed with unaccustomed helplessness. Surely, there had to something she could do. There must be a commission she could complain to—but he was the commission. Megan scrapped the commission idea. A letter writing campaign—but to whom? The academic journals were his oyster, he their purest pearl, *sans peur* and *sans raproche*, the Galahad of the Ivory Tower. Consciousness raising sessions—but her consciousness was raised. She didn't see how it could possibly be raised any more. She had spent years telling other women how to empower themselves; indeed, that was what the conference in New Jersey had been all about. Surely, she couldn't be anything like those pathetic women who allowed their husbands to abuse them, crying helplessness, or those girls who let themselves be shuffled off into brothels, not realizing that all they needed to do was stand up for themselves and assert their individual rights.

She knew her worth as a rights-bearing individual. She had read all the international treaties. She had even drafted a few model provisions, including one recommending mandatory reeducation programs for women in third world countries and the westerly sort of American state, to alert them to their rights as autonomous individuals. Why, there was recourse for everything, if only these poor, benighted women were shown where to look for it.

Yet, here she was, caught as surely as any frumpy-haired housewife stuck between a beer and a barca lounger as her unshaven spouse bore down upon her like an outtake from a Tennessee Williams production.

"I think I see." The words scratched against her throat.

"Good."

"It's all about practice rather than theory." Megan's voice grew stronger as she continued. "It's easy for me to sit there and say what people should do or not do, but you've just demonstrated for me just how hard it is for a student to refute an advance from a faculty member."

"Mm-hmm." Agnelli's face was a study in shadow.

"I see what you're trying to prove—it was really very effective—but I still think Cliff's case is different...."

"Megan." The sound of her name silenced her instantly. "Must you?" he said wearily.

It was the fatigue that convinced her, the hideous weariness of a man defeated by his own nature.

Megan's throat felt very dry. "I prefer it to the alternative," she said.

When Agnelli answered, his voice was meticulously cultured and dry as the law. "Since you are so fond of memos, I suggest you prepare one for me."

"A memo," Megan repeated flatly.

For all she knew, memo might be a hideous sexual double entendre, a female equivalent to the masculine brief. Memo even sounded like mammo, as in mammary and mammogram, and from there it was only a short hop to breasts, the classic object of male objectification of the female form.

Agnelli's eyes, however, remained scrupulously above the neck, as he tilted his head and considered, fingers steepled in time honored professorial fashion. "Twenty pages... that should be enough space. You may go over slightly if you feel a pressing need, but do try to keep your argument concise. I'd like it double-spaced, with one inch margins, and pagination in the lower left hand corner."

"Twenty pages on what?"

"I'd like to see twenty pages arguing the merits of a new paradigm in sexual harassment cases. How was it that you phrased it?"

In that fuzzy borderline where the Socratic crossed into the rhetorical, Megan couldn't tell whether she was supposed to reply or not. It was the sort of definitional problem that tended to get the more eager sorts of 1Ls glared at by their professors, as they launched their arms into the air to answer, interrupting an otherwise seamless narrative. Professors never appreciated that.

Agnelli went smoothly on, delivering his set piece like a Greek orator in the agora. "Insulating without being infantalizing. Very nice. Let's see that spun out, shall we? I want a twenty page defense of your arguments on behalf of Cliff. And, by extension, your arguments on behalf of *this*."

With that same self-deprecating smile, the smile that graced that dust jacket of all of his books and simpered modestly down from the walls of Pound Hall, he extended a hand to Megan, palm up. It was a large palm, callused from holding protest signs, bearing the scars from a 70's summer working in a mining camp in the Appalachians ("Professor becomes one with workers!"), seared and seamed with the testimony of thirty years of devotion to worthy causes.

Megan made no move to take it. "My argument doesn't extend that far."

"You won't know unless you sit down and write it, now, will you?"

"I won't write it. I *can't* write it. For, you, of all people…."

"That is your decision to make. I would advise you, however," the Acting Dean continued, in the same, kindly tones, "not to make it precipitately. I shall expect the memo Thursday evening—in person. Goodnight, Megan. Although this matter of Mr.

Walker is undeniably sordid, I am grateful that it has brought you to my attention."

A day ago, Megan might have said the same.

Turning as stiffly as a Barbie doll, Megan pushed on the glass door. Her arms were rubbery, as uncooperative as if she had just put in an hour of heavy weightlifting at Hemenway gym. Achieving the hallway, Megan walked numbly towards the elevator, not looking back. Somewhere behind her, Agnelli still sat in his office, like the spider in the nursery rhyme. *Come into my parlor, said the spider to the fly.* Megan had always mocked at the naïvete of the fly. Even at three, she knew better.

Her decision to make. The illusion of autonomy stung more than outright coercion. It wasn't a choice, it was blackmail dressed in the language of self-determination. Choose his way, and she jettisoned her principles; pick the other, and she damned Cliff.

Well, Megan reminded herself, as she hurried towards Harkness Commons, Cliff had already damned himself, by taking up with Julia. She really couldn't be held accountable for that. Naturally, there was no question of her taking Dean Agnelli up on his offer. Cliff would just have to understand that.

The real problem, though, wasn't Cliff, but Agnelli.

Just a week ago, she had helped distribute flyers throughout the women's bathrooms. There, on the inside of the bathroom stalls where their captive audience would be forced to read and reflect, she had posted, "Rape: No Longer the Silent Crime." Below, the text had urged women to speak out, promising support, counseling, protection, "Because if you don't, he WILL do it again. YOU can stop the conspiracy of silence. Just call...."

If she didn't speak out, she would keeping the conspiracy of silence, while, like a bloated spider, Agnelli spun his webs in the security of his borrowed office, waiting for the next unwary fly to blunder into his net. How many women had he used, as he had tried to use her? How many "dinners" had he had, how many memoranda had he lingered over in the privacy of his Brattle Street bedroom?

Megan struggled with the glass door that led into the Hark; always heavy, today it felt deliberately weighted against her.

Unlike its lunchtime bustle, the Hark was largely deserted. To her left, the plate glass windows of the Law School Coop, the tiny little bookstore set into one side of the Hark, were dark, its treasure trove of study aids and bubble gum pink HLS t-shirts locked up for the night. Even the flat-screen television set into the wall, designed to announce the day's happenings (nothing so mundane as posters for the privileged ranks of America's intellectual elite) had gone blank, relieved of its daily burden. On her right, a smattering of people sprawled with their laptops in the sunken lounge, as still and silent as figures from Sleeping Beauty's castle. With the small café closed, the two friendly women who worked there gone home for the night, the area felt as forlorn as a midnight gas station. The only sign of life was the occasional click of the keys, but even their clatter took on a subdued tone, muffled by the twilight. The windowed walls that let in the light by day also let in the dark by night.

Upstairs the lights would be brighter and her editorial board would be waiting. Megan hurried up the ramp to the second floor, designed, like the campus itself, to take twice as long as a normal flight of stairs by doubling back on itself. Theoretically, it was supposed to serve the needs of the handicapped, but the angle was steep enough to repel any but the most adventurous, Social Darwinism applied to the law school cafeteria.

In the blandly beige wasteland of the Hark dining hall, three women and one male made various gestures of greeting as Megan hurried across the room to join them. They were as unlikely a group as the gang in *The Breakfast Club*, and constituted along oddly similar lines: the preppy, the princess, the rebel, and the nerd.

"I like your suit," offered Amanda, her Alabama drawl extending the words long enough to give Megan time to yank out a chair and insert herself into it.

Everything about Amanda was muted, from her blurred voice to her snub nose to the pastel shades she favored for everything from her pink sneakers to her collection of candy-colored tank-tops. Even her soft brown hair appeared as though it had lost its original color from too many washings. With a mind as mild as her features, Amanda's presence at both law school and a feminist organization was a mystery best explained by one word: regionalism. The law school liked to boast of the geographical diversity of the student body. In her local college, Amanda had spearheaded the radical women's movement, leading an initiative to get rid of the long-running school tradition of separate sections in the bleachers of the football stadium for those with who came with dates and those girls who came alone. "It's just plain mean to make those girls who can't get a date feel even worse about it," was how she put it when asked.

Robyn, on the other hand, couldn't understand why Amanda had bothered with small fry, like space in the bleachers, when what she ought to have done was picketed the entire football team. Football, after all, was a chauvinistic ritual of aggression that only fueled the delusions and the libido of the budding members of the military-industrial conspiracy. It had to be a conspiracy; Robyn would settle for nothing so bland as a complex.

Besides, complexes had been invented by a man. They were clearly an attempt by the weak-willed Viennese male to subjugate and contain the great goddess that lived within all women—corsets for the mind as well as the body.

Proving that she hadn't succumbed to media myths about the female body, Robyn's belly bulged over the waistband of her low-rise jeans, and excess flesh surged over the tight elastic of her tank top. Her signature crop-tops and hip-huggers gave whole new meaning to letting it all hang out. Her hair, a relic of Second Wave Feminism, exploded in full frizz from under a folded bandana, like the before half of a conditioner commercial. There was a rumor that she secretly curled it to achieve the proper aesthetic of ethnic abandon, but that, so far, had yet to be substantiated. No one dared ask. Grooming was not a subject one brought up with Robyn, who viewed discussion of any body part that wasn't societally taboo as inherently counter-revolutionary. The clitoris was a safe topic; hair care was not.

A white piece of paper had been taped around the circumference of Robyn's water bottle. In hand-lettered capitals, it read "Make a Revolution Every Day."

The sentiment had always struck Megan as profoundly wasteful. How, after all, could you ever get anything accomplished if you were frittering your time away between multiple revolutions, rather than focusing on just one?

"We started without you," announced Carter, whose small gold hoops and bulldozer manners proclaimed her boarding school background as surely as her ribbon belt. She consulted her clipboard. "We've already dealt with the order for this year's t-shirts, letters of protest to three Middle Eastern governments, and refreshments for this Saturday's subcite."

"About the t-shirts," drawled Amanda.

"Yes, Amanda, we will have some made in pink, as long as the manufacturer agrees to make it an ironic pink. Now, we were up to Item Four: our new name. Law and Gender, or Gender and the Law?"

Scorning Robert's Rules of Order as a male construct, Robyn thumped her water bottle against the plastic tabletop and seized the floor. "By putting law before gender, you validate the centuries of oppression inflicted by the bias of masculine legislation. We need to put gender before law, in every way. You see? You have to make law the instrument for social change rather than society the instrument of the law."

"That's so Critical Legal Studies," drawled Carter, lazily twisting her long blonde hair into a knot and securing it by driving a pen through it. "Been there, done that." Having dismissed the efforts of a generation of legal scholars with one casual hair-do, she yanked out the pen and shook out her hair. "Anyone else have any ideas? Megan?"

"Um…. Would you guys mind if we detoured to something else for a moment?" The Journal of Women and the Law was run along strictly cooperative lines, which meant that every demand had to be phrased as a request. "It's really important."

Some people cooperated better than others. Carter fixed her with the stare that launched a thousand Junior Leagues. "Then you should have thought of that before we set the agenda. We can't have people thinking that organization is purely a male quality."

"No," agreed Megan, brushing back her hair with an unsteady hand. "But what if... what if a male professor you really respected...."

"Oh, God," groaned Amanda. In her generous diction, the Deity acquired an extra syllable. "Not a hypothetical! Don't we get enough of those in class?"

Robyn pounced. "Don't you mean, O Goddess? In perpetuating the myth of the masculine deity, you're—"

Carter tapped her pen impatiently against the table. The matriarchal tribal council was called to order. "If you all don't mind, we still have a name to change. I believe Doug had something he wanted to add to the discussion?"

Doug, their token male, straightened his scrawny frame and tried to look insightful yet respectful, succeeding only in appearing mildly dyspeptic. Doug had come late to feminism; his epiphany had occurred after discovering, via Facebook, that Carter was on the editorial board. His road to Damascus consisted of a crash course in the feminist teachings, courtesy of Books on Tape.

"I suggest," ventured Doug, carefully employing a neutral verb, "that we consider going with something that does more to celebrate the achievements women have, er, achieved over the past few decades. How about something like 'A Celebration of Women and the Law'?"

He looked hopefully at Carter.

Carter, who only dated squash players, obliterated his hopes with an oscillation of her earrings. "Too Madonna."

Doug's shoulders sagged under his neon green t-shirt.

Amanda giggled. "We could use her as our theme song."

"You find this funny?" demanded Robyn. "I'm sorry; there is nothing funny about two thousand years of oppression."

Megan was more concerned with twenty minutes ago.

"Look, I really think you ought to—" Megan cut in.

"Thanks, Meg." Carter took over. "Come on, all, focus. We're not using 'women' in the title anymore, because we don't want to imply that this is purely a female issue. Gender goes both ways, right?"

"Right!" seconded Doug.

Carter gave him an okay-weirdo look. Like Gonzo, Doug dwelt post-gender, in the realm of the neutered. "So the big question is Law and Gender, or Gender and Law. I'm for Law and Gender, since this is a legal journal, and we want people to take us seriously as legal minds, not as gendered beings. Robyn is for Gender and Law"—Robyn's cheeks bulged as she took a corroborative swig from her revolutionary water bottle; Carter had masterfully timed her moment so Robyn would have no chance to charge in and elaborate— "and so is Amanda."

"It can't hurt to be earlier in the alphabet," explained Amanda earnestly to Megan, twining a strand of hair around one finger. "This even puts us ahead all of the journals that begin with Journal!" Megan didn't have the energy to point out to her that the *Journal of Gender and Law* still began with J.

"Doug?"

Doug had a glaze-eyed look that suggested he was running through his alphabet to determine whether "G" did, in fact, come before "J." When Carter spoke, he snapped to.

"Law and Gender."

Where his goddess went, so went he.

"Megan?

"Can I just run something by you first?"

"Megan." Carter tilted her head to one side. "We've been through this already. You're the one who came up with the whole agenda idea, so let's stick to it, okay? Whatever it is, we can just put it on next week's agenda and deal with it then."

"Carter—"

"We just don't have time right now to deal with an extra issue. Amanda has a pilates class at 8:00, Robin has a sit-in, and I have a date." The date was clearly not with Doug, who went from manful to mournful in an instant. "Next week. All right?"

"Whatever." Next week would be too late. And why would they believe her? She barely believed herself. Agnelli, of all people! "Never mind."

Carter was still looking at her expectantly. "Hello. Megan?"

"Oh, Law and Gender."

She and Carter had already discussed the new title at length last Friday, in complete agreement about the necessity of its fundamentally legal character and of out-voting Robin. The outcome had been pre-determined before the debate began.

"Law and Gender carries." Carter tipped her pen like a gavel, an entirely unconscious holdover from her college debating society. "Don't forget, we're holding our first mass subcite on Saturday. 10:00, Langdell South. Don't be late. Amanda will be picking up the coffee and doughnuts, and Robin will be making reminder calls Friday night to all the line editors. Got that? Great. See you Saturday."

Megan marveled at the mundanity of it. Across the law school campus, girls in Harvard fleeces were annotating their textbooks in color-coded magic marker or taking advantage of the wireless internet in the library to click back and forth on instant message, mocking their fellows and exchanging the latest on Brad, Angelina, and judicial nominations; boys in Georgetown t-shirts (or Penn or Duke) were hoisting weights in the lower level of the gym, while above them earnest girls in ponytails and sports bras pounded away on the treadmills and bounced up and down on the elliptical trainers. In the red brick apartment houses lining Mass Ave, people were cooking dinner and talking on the phone and fretting about Moot Court trials.

None of them realized that the world had cracked off its axis and tilted to one side.

And on Saturday morning, a group of fresh-faced 1Ls would show up at the Langdell South bright and early, ready to sacrifice one of the last warm days of the semester to sit inside the cluttered Reference Room and painstakingly check a list of citations from a five page fragment of an article against an editorial symbol sheet, a shelf of reference books, and the subciters' Bible, the

Blue Book, which was to legal writing what the Chicago Manual of Style was to budding grammarians. The subcites invariably took the whole day, but they provided the ultimate reward. Not wisdom, since no one subciter ever had possession of more than seven pages of an eighty page article, but that far more valuable prize: an extra bullet point on one's resume.

A mere twenty-four hours ago, the subcite had been a source of anxiety and caffeine consumption. Megan had fretted over preparing the lists of editorial marks; she had debated intensely with Carter over the relative merits of bran muffins as opposed to doughnut holes (workers fueled with sugar might work more quickly, but those fed with fiber worked longer); and she had spent a good deal of energy wheedling a draft of an overdue article from a senior professor who claimed his muse was on sabbatical and couldn't be bothered with deadlines.

Megan yearned for the comforting triviality of it all.

Slinging her J. Crew bag over her shoulder, Carter tapped Megan on the arm. "Are you okay? It's not like you to be late, and I've never seen you this unfocused."

"Well, actually…."

"Fuck!" Carter frowned at the clock above Megan's head. "Is it that late? We'll coffee later this week, okay?" Carter mimed tossing back the contents of a Starbucks cup. From long habit, her fingers perfectly replicated the circumference of a grande latte, complete with cardboard holder.

"Sure," said Megan, but Carter was already blazing off towards the stairs. Feminism was one thing, being late for a date quite another.

She could try calling Carter later… but she had a fairly good hunch that Carter wouldn't be answering her phone. Not if the date went as intended. This one not only played squash, he rowed crew, a sure way to Carter's bed. She claimed it was the resulting arm muscles. Megan thought it had more to do with a certain boarding school musk, the scent of old socks and older money all wrapped up in the same gym bag.

Megan couldn't quite bring herself to go home. Going home would mean a cessation of activity. Cessation of activity meant thought. And thought meant… things she didn't want to think about. Rachel would undoubtedly be out—Monday night was "Sex in the City" night for the female members of Lincoln's Inn—and Megan didn't particularly want to be alone with herself.

She would stop off in the BSA office and pick up those papers to grade. Even grading would be a welcome relief. Grateful for an errand to run, any errand, she wove her way around the abandoned metal tables outside the Hark.

Even though the night had grown chilly, she took the longer way into Pound Hall, walking the length of the brick patio, towards the side door tucked away next to the empty table where the coffee urns usually stood. She didn't want to have to face the long row of faculty photos that lined the hallway of the first floor of Pound like so many Byzantine saints, Agnelli prominently featured among them.

She must have misunderstood somehow. What had happened, after all? An invitation to dinner. A request for a memo. There was nothing particularly offensive in either, even by Robyn's draconian standards. All that rendered it otherwise was a certain twist to his words. It had been a long day; she had been frazzled after her interviews, and her long trek to and from the Charles.

The more she tried to pin the exact phrases down, the faster they wriggled away. The scene was already misting in her memory.

How could she prove her claim to anyone else, when she couldn't even prove it to herself?

Instead of turning right, towards the BSA office, she found herself instead rotating left, towards the cursory lounge area in front of the elevators, and the OCS office just beyond. In spite of the late hour, the door of the OCS office stood ajar. The transparent film of light spreading across a triangle of carpet signaled human occupation. It might just be the janitor, engaged in his nightly rounds, but Megan changed course anyway, making for the light like Robinson Crusoe with a cruise ship in view.

Mr. Friar had asked her to report on her meeting with Dean Agnelli....

CHAPTER SEVEN

The Duke: *"Be absolute for death....*
Reason thus with life:
If I do lose thee, I do lose a thing
That none but fools would keep....
Happy thou art not,
For what thou hast not, still thou striv'st to get
And what thou hast, forget'st...
And when thou art old and rich,
Thou has neither heat, affection, limb, nor beauty,
To make thy riches pleasant."

Claudio: *"I humbly thank you.*
To sue to live, I find I seek to die."
   -- III, i, 5-8, 21-23, 36-38, 41-43

Bob Friar's office was too small for two grown men.

Cliff sat hunched in the one guest chair, a sideless, nearly backless affair held together by three screws and the fact that there was no room for it to tip over. Since two chairs would have brought their knees into proximity unbecoming two heterosexual men, Friar had elected to stand, if standing it could be called. Both hands braced behind him, Friar leaned against the precarious ledge that ran around three sides of his cubbyhole and doubled as a desk. The windowless room, clothed in the silence of the deserted campus, felt less like an office, and more like a confessional.

Friar had suggested that they meet after hours, and Cliff had been grateful for his tact. After hours meant anonymity. After hours meant not having to fight his way through the various protests and counter-protests that clustered in the piazza in front of the Hark. Like unions, student organizations tended to keep well-defined working hours. Causes were well and good as long as they didn't conflict with prime time television.

Like most of the faculty, Cliff spent a great deal of breath bemoaning student apathy. It was practically a requirement, like teaching basic classes and writing ponderous law review articles that no one ever read, except the harried article editor who skimmed it on her way to another bullet point on her resume. The uneducable in pursuit of the inconsequential.

Right now, Cliff could have done with a bit more student apathy.

His amorous imbroglio had done more to electrify the campus than the last presidential election. It certainly reached more constituencies. The HLS branch of the God Squad ("Sinners our Specialty!"), a loose alliance of Baptists, Methodists, First Day Adventists, Second Day Adventists, Low Church Lutherans, Any Church Anti-Trinitarians, and militant Mormons, had held a Pray-In for his soul and that of the innocent young girl he had led astray. He had even been featured in their internet newsletter, "Bulletins from Babylon," next to a rather graphic woodcut illustration of the last days of Sodom.

On the other side of the spectrum, the Gay and Lesbian Students Organization had placed a hotly worded editorial in the most recent issue of *The Record*, taking him to task for promoting the heteronormative paradigm by committing his discretions with someone of the opposite gender. And even the discovery that Julia was one-tenth Native American had done nothing to discourage the wrath of the various minority groups who were crying discrimination.

He had gone, in the space of one fatal date, from a mildly popular lecturer with a promising career to a bigoted homophobe destined to burn in hell.

Lincoln's Inn, on the other hand, had voted him an honorary member. A delegation, swaying slightly from the aftereffects of their last kegger, had appeared at his office to solemnly present him with a key to the Inn, and a mumbled, "Scamming on the students—yeah!"

He knew they should have rented a DVD.

At the time, it had all seemed so harmless. That was one of the dangers of legal training; he could argue any side with equal facility, whether it had intrinsic merit or not. In this case, it hadn't even taken much mental slight of hand. Julia wasn't a dewy-eyed little twenty-two year old, and he—or, at least, so he would prefer to think—wasn't a perverted old lecher, even if his hairline was beginning to recede a bit under the rigors of an intellectual regime.

Julia had been only a year behind him at Yale, class of '98 to his '97. They hadn't known each other back in their bulldog days. His world had revolved around the

Political Union and the Yale College Dems, hers around the bio labs and the Yale Glee Club. She had been in Pierson, he in Calhoun. Like the solar system, university life moved in dozens of separate orbits, moving in parallel, but never meeting, a world of worlds contained within the casual rubric of college. They had probably passed each other a dozen times on Cross Campus, bumped trays at lunchtime in Commons, and elbowed past each other through the drunken Friday throngs in the God Quad.

After graduation, he had gone off to England for a year, to Cambridge, to study political philosophy and capsize punts on the Cam. She had gone straight to the other Cambridge, for a bio degree at MIT. All those years, while he had been in law school, writing practice briefs and attending avant garde theatrical productions at the ART, she had been just two stops down the Red Line at MIT, dissecting small rodents and eating cheap Middle Eastern food in Central Square.

With the intellectual property boom, lawyers with a science background were suddenly in hot demand. When legal recruiters came to MIT, Julia—by then, Dr. Julia, in pursuit of a post-doc—had decided to throw in her petrie dishes and lob in an application to law school. On a lark, as she put it, mocking the faux English slang that Cliff had picked up during his year in Cambridge (more to do with re-runs of *Brideshead* than anything he had actually heard in the Fellows Common Room). Only Julia would claim to have gone to Harvard Law School on a lark. She was, thought Cliff, one of the most terrifyingly intelligent people he knew. She sliced through academic disciplines as though they were butter. No nonsense about being either a science person or a humanities person for her; if it was put in front of her, she could do it.

She was also, as she admitted to Cliff, rather sick of dissecting mice at minimum wage. If someone wanted to pay her absurd amounts of money to sit in a sterile office and spool out words, she was right there.

That was another thing he liked about Julia. Her frankness. No pretense about legal epiphanies or saving the world. No pretense at all.

It might have served them better if she had.

It was only last summer that the chance collision had occurred. A statistical probability, Julia had laughingly called it, after ten years of near misses. A mutual friend, Branford '98, in the Political Union with him, in the Glee Club with her, had thrown a summer drinks party at his apartment in Back Bay. By then, she was already admitted to law school, already had her section assignment—in his section.

Naturally, they didn't put that together until the following morning.

Over croissants and coffee, with the summer sun slanting across the scratched hardwood of his living room floor, the coincidence had seemed more amusing than alarming, a "can you believe?" to be tossed back and forth, with incredulous smiles and much shaking of heads. Amused. They had actually been amused.

Lazily, over subsequent dates, they had discussed the possibility of her transferring sections. But it wasn't like switching a class; the section compositions were worked out with Byzantine complexity, so many women and minorities to the mix. To move from one section to the other required upheavals of the earth that made Pompeii look tame in comparison. The law school, in all its wisdom, had long ago determined that the terrors of legal education were best faced with an unchanging band of fellows, a military squadron with textbooks. The eighty members of a section took all their first year classes together, only vaguely aware of the other six sections doing likewise. In seven sections they went to class, took their exams, and got drunk off their ass.

All her classes were based around that one section assignment, all her future colleagues determined, all her books bought. To move would mark her out as a scarlet woman from day one, to be whispered about among the sections as "that girl who had to switch sections because she was sleeping with a professor." Just which professor she happened to be sleeping with would probably vary as the rumor moved along. Cliff wasn't suitably high profile to make good gossip, so Julia was more likely to have her name paired with a series of blameless octogenarians, who were more likely to sleep with the galleys of their latest textbooks than their students.

It wasn't fair to make Julia start out with that sort of stigma, just because she had the poor taste to want to continue dating him.

At least, that was how they rationalized it to themselves.

Besides, when it came down to it, he wouldn't grade any of her papers, or have anything to do with her daily progress. Julia was in Megan's subsection, and if anyone walked the straight and narrow, it was Megan. She could turn a boulevard into a tightrope. There was lecture once a week, but he failed to see how any hint of impropriety could make its way through so impersonal a vehicle as a lecture.

True, there had been that time Julia had raised her hand in class. He had called on her, squinting at her name card with exaggerated care, "Miss… Kemp."

"Kemp-*ee*," she corrected him with all due sobriety, but a little light danced in her eyes, an ion of inebriation crackling its way from the back row to the podium.

He conducted the rest of the class in a punch-drunk haze.

Everyone always talked about the danger to the student, but what about the danger to the professor? For hours afterwards, he couldn't have told his Marbury from his Madison. If anyone had asked him where to find the correct form for a statutory citation, he probably would have replied, "In Julia's eyes." If there was a power imbalance in their relationship, it ran exclusively in the opposite direction.

He was doing it again, Cliff realized. Justifying. Pleading with an invisible advocate.

If he had to do it all again, would he choose his job or Julia?

The Lady or the Tiger?

At the time, the dichotomy just hadn't arisen. Even if they had been caught, their peccadillo was so perfectly plausible. It would take a martinet with iced-latte running through his veins to find fault, and Dean Arden was known as a reasonable man. Far greater infractions had been deftly swept aside with a nudge and a wink. Cliff could point to half a dozen examples. The assistant professor who had taken up with a 2L, the senior faculty member who married a graduating 3L, the visiting professor who dated an LLM…. Both visiting professors and LLM's being the protozoa of the law school food chain, no one had accorded that latter instance much attention, the primary reaction seeming to be that they deserved each other. How else was one expected to get through the long, Cambridge winter?

That, of course, had been pre-Agnelli.

Cliff had to clear his throat before he could speak. "My chances aren't good, are they?"

Friar's face was the sort of kindly mask associated with television doctors delegated with the news of improbable illnesses. "Have you ever considered a career in public service?"

"Public service," Cliff repeated flatly.

It was a career death sentence.

Public service meant joining the ranks of earnest civil servants who earned less in ten years than their education had cost them in one. He had looked down on them before from his protected perch as a Supreme Court Clerk, watching them bustle about, perpetually harried, condemned to cheap coffee and cheaper suits, percolating downwards from one small public interest group to another, zombies in the graveyard of lost lawyers.

That sort of thing didn't happen to the Editor-in-Chief of the Harvard Law Review and winner of the Sears Prize. He had even been voted Most Likely to Be A Supreme Court Justice by the Harvard Law School class of 2001. That had to count for something.

"There must be some other way. If the old Dean...."

"The old Dean isn't here. Even if he were," he added, "the best he would have been able to arrange would be a year's sabbatical to let it all blow over."

"Do you think...?"

"No." Friar's voice was kindly, but firm, an antidote to hope. "Cliff, there's no point in tormenting yourself with false expectations."

"You make it sound so final," muttered Cliff. "Perhaps some compromise could be reached... some sort of deal. If someone were to speak to the Acting Dean...."

"Have you ever known Arthur Agnelli to back down?"

There was only one possible answer to that. Cliff didn't need to voice it. It was written all over his face.

Friar wagged a finger at him. "Don't take it so hard. There are many perfectly viable options outside of the academy."

"Are there?" Cliff realized he sounded skeptical, and, worse than that, sullen. But however nicely Friar tried to phrase it, it all amounted to the same thing. He was being expelled.

"Think of all the drawbacks to the academic life. You must have bemoaned them in the past. Everyone does. The long hours, the low pay, the lack of worldly recognition."

"That's like saying death isn't so bad because life is tough," Cliff objected despairingly.

Friar chuckled. "No one is trying to shove you off this mortal coil, Cliff. You have to try to put it all in perspective—that way, no matter what happens, you won't be disappointed. Try to think of the wider world as an opportunity, not expulsion from Eden. There are no Edens anymore, not even in the ivory tower."

Cliff regarded him dubiously. Not Eden, perhaps, but what other job would allow you to work for one hour at a time, three days a week, and laud you for doing so?

"When you look at it," Friar mused, "an academic appointment isn't all that much of a prize. Your friends who went into private practice have money with which to soothe themselves. The public interest crowd have their shiny haloes. But what do you have? Nothing but the satisfaction of shaping America's future legal minds."

"What's wrong with that?"

Friar smiled understandingly. "It sounds grand when you sign up for it, doesn't it? We all have images of being Professor Kingsolver or doing Mr. Chips one better." He countered Cliff's unguarded expression of surprise with a slightly wry smile. "Yes, I did some teaching myself in my day. I wasn't always as you see me now. That Mr. Chips image only lasts until you actually teach your first class. You know what I'm talking about don't you?"

Reluctantly, Cliff nodded.

"The DVDs on their computer screens, the on-line shopping during class, the whispering, the snickering, the instant messaging. You can never tell whether they're laughing at what you just said or whether they're just poking fun at that poor nerd in the third row. They don't care. They don't want their minds shaped. They just want to get their degrees and get out."

Cliff couldn't deny the truth of that. The job-hunting process, as strictly orchestrated as Edwardian courtship rituals, began in September of the 2L year. By November, students already had their summer jobs in hand. Barring extreme disaster, those summer jobs were guaranteed to mature into proper job offers come August, simply by virtue of the passage of time.

Three months into their second year, their future was assured. They might as well not be in law school anymore—but law firms tended to be a bit persnickety about their employees actually having degree in hand when they started work. It would look bad on the firm website, otherwise. As to how the law student filled that remaining year and a half of school time, neither the firm nor the student particularly cared. Tales of students jetting off to Vegas for the entirety of their 3L year were only part urban myth.

Friar's voice continued, a hypnotic burr on the verge of Cliff's consciousness. "They get out. You don't. You sit here, season in and season out, while your students come and go. Their lives are filled with excitement and opportunity; yours is mired in stasis. Why do you think academics spend so much of their time jetting about to conferences? They need to provide an illusion of activity, of action. You stand in the same classrooms, teach the same material, winter after Cambridge winter."

Put that way, it was enough to make a man want to slit his wrists.

Cliff shook his head to clear it. "Maybe you're right," he mumbled. "Maybe I do need to get out of here."

Friar dealt him a fatherly slap on the back. "That's my boy! Look at the opportunity, not the demerit. Come back tomorrow, and I'll have a list of prospects prepared for you. Would you like to look exclusively at public service, or shall I make a few discreet calls to some of the larger firms?"

"I don't care." Nothing really mattered anymore. Nothing at all. He was like the Great Gatsby, doomed always to be on the wrong side of the harbor. Or was that the other character?

He couldn't even get a simple literary allusion right. He was useless. Hopeless. He didn't know what Julia saw in him—or what she would see in him, stripped of his career and his future. Julia was so forward-thinking, so matter-of-fact. She had mastered two careers. He couldn't even manage one.

At thirty-one, he was a has-been.

"Both, then," said Friar, making a slight notation on his pad.

"Fine."

A slight slither of ink on the page, and there it all went. The tenure-track job, the media consultations, the scholarly articles, the eventual appellate court appointment. He could hear the door slamming shut on his ambitions, in surround sound.

Looking up, Cliff squinted over his shoulder, out the door of Friar's cubicle, into the main office. Unless he was really losing it—which was definitely an option—that had been a real door, not just a sound effect of the mind.

"Hello?" a familiar voice called. "Mr. Friar?"

CHAPTER EIGHT

"Claudio: *Ay, but to die, and go we know not where,*
To lie in cold obstruction and to rot
…'tis too horrible!
The weariest and most loathed worldly life
That age, ache, penury, and imprisonment
Can lay on nature is a paradise
To what we fear of death.
…Sweet sister, let me live."

Isabella: *O you beast,*
O faithless coward, O dishonest wretch!
Wilt thou be made a man out of my vice?
…Take my defiance,
Die, perish!
…   I'll pray a thousand prayers for they death,
No word to save thee."
        --III, i, 118-119, 129-138, 143-144, 146-147.

Cliff was out of his chair and halfway across the main room before the final syllable had left Megan's lips.

"Cliff?" She blinked at him in a way that had nothing to do with the uneven light. "I didn't know you were here."

She was dressed for interviews, he noticed, in a dark suit and snagged stockings, with a leather portfolio sticking unevenly out of her ubiquitous tote. The echo of interview season reminded Cliff forcibly of his own rapidly dwindling employment options.

Without pausing for the amenities, he blurted out, "I heard you spoke to Dean Agnelli?"

He hated himself for the pleading note in his voice, but it was too late for that. No matter how bad Bob Friar made the academy sound, when it came right down to it, he would beg or plead or grovel or do anything he had to do to get his job back. A life in public service was too grim to contemplate.

"I did." Megan's countenance offered no encouragement. "I'm sorry."

The words hit Cliff like a blow to the stomach.

"That bad?" He tried to smile, but it came out crooked.

Megan didn't even try. "Worse."

He hadn't thought there could be a worse. Other, of course, than Julia's leaving him, and that he expected momentarily. What use, after all, could a vibrant woman have for a has-been like him? As a power couple, they made sense. As he was now, the most he could contribute to the relationship were dishwashing services. The ability to make esoteric pronouncements about Supreme Court jurisprudence did not go far outside of the academy.

What could possibly be worse? Had they unearthed an obscure seventeenth century law pertaining to professors in the academy? Somewhere on the crumbling rolls might be an *Iniunction Contrarye to Fornicacion* with one's students; there was, after all, still a law on the books from that same time permitting Harvard College professors, if they so desired, to pasture their cows on Cambridge Common. To Cliff's knowledge, no one had tried it for well over a century, but the provision was still good law, as were dozens others that lingered more because they were quaint— and because it would be more trouble for the legislature to expunge them than to keep them—than for any other reason. Agnelli would be just the man to root around colonial charters for a punishment that would suit his puritanical standards. The early settlers had been inventive sorts. Cliff wouldn't be surprised to find himself set in the stocks with a sign about his neck (Beholde Ye Olde Lechere) and pelted with warm cow dug, before being run out of town on a rail.

The legal faculty would probably dub it Performative Punishment. They would ooh and aah about community involvement and the interactive nature of justice as they took turns lobbing their balls of dung.

More realistically, Agnelli might be planning to demand that Cliff be expelled not only from the school but from the Bar itself, the guild-like organization that controlled the activities of all American attorneys. In the legal profession, disbarment had something of the same effect as excommunication in the medieval church; flung from the fold, the sinner was shunned by the faithful and banned from all sacred practices. In short, he was damned. Even public service would be beyond his reach.

Legal Ethics not being Cliff's field, he couldn't remember whether professor student relations were grounds of disbarment. There was something about lawyers not sleeping with their clients, a provision generally honored in the breech, but did a student really count as a client? He could come up with arguments going either way. It would make a great First Year Lawyering memo assignment.

Only he wouldn't be teaching First Year Lawyering or anything else. Ever again.

"How worse?" he asked Megan apprehensively.

Megan looked grim. "You don't want to know."

And that was that, he supposed. Sticking his hands in his pockets, Cliff said awkwardly, "Thanks for trying. That was really decent of you."

"I enjoyed working for you."

The phrase had the solemn knell of a eulogy. She was even wearing black. Cliff's own blue Oxford shirt and khackis seemed positively frivolous in contrast. Dearly beloved, we are gathered here today to mourn the career of one Cliff Walker....

Cliff made an effort to pull himself together. "Thanks. The feeling is mutual."

Megan looked at him anxiously. "Did you ever think of teaching undergrad? Like in a Poli Sci or a Gov department?"

"I'd need a PhD for that." Cliff gazed unseeingly at one of the bright posters on the wall. It advertised a Legal Services cruise to Jamaica with the legend, *Improve your Resume and your Tan!* In smaller print, the poster explained that there would be seminars on immigration law, human rights law, and post-colonial theory, as well as a nightly luau on the festival deck. Arts and Sciences professors didn't get those sorts of perks. Without any bargaining power in the real world—what marketable skills, after all, did one have as a Doctor of Philosophy?—they were expected to work long hours for pay that wouldn't cover their T fare. And that was assuming they were among the lucky who actually got a job at the end of their decade of study. "Seven more years of school? I don't think I could do it. Not anymore."

"There's always prep school," suggested Megan helpfully.

Cliff shook his head to ward off further suggestions, before Megan had him teaching pre-law at a New York nursery school. He'd find himself at the 92nd Street Y teaching Tiny Torts and Contracts for the Under Two's, with pretentious toddlers asking him about the pros and cons of negotiating a long term lease on the right half of the sandbox.

Teaching high school… oh, God. How had it come to this? How in the hell would he be able to show his face at his tenth year reunion at Yale?

"Don't worry," he said unconvincingly, sticking his hands in his pockets. "I'll think of something. At least I know it's nobody's fault but my own. I got myself into this. It's only fair."

It didn't make him feel any better when Megan nodded.

"Assumption of risk, that's what it was. I knew the risk, and I dated her anyway. I brought it all on myself. Oh, God." The Arkansas accent he had worked so hard to suppress over long years at Yale emerged, turning his cry to the deity into a nasal yawp.

He had thought he could get away, remake himself, expunge the regionalism from his soul as thoroughly as he had from his voice and appearance. He was of the Northeast these days, of the coffee house and the wine tasting and the cool blue of a political pundit's map. Not for him the overheated red of the Bible-thumping regions of the South. He chose chill; argument iced over with reason, like his wine, like the river, like the cooler than cool music that crooned from the speakers of Inman Square coffee houses.

But no matter how blue he colored himself, in moments of distress, the twang came back. Like Banquo's ghost, like Richard's victims, like the bloodstain of a British ghost story. It came back, to point a long finger at him and cry, "J'Accuse!"

What use was it that he could think that in French? What use was it that he could come up with not one, but two examples of Shakespearean hauntings? Under a veneer of Derrida and Fouccault, the red rubbed through. All those years at Yale, at Cambridge, and at Harvard were as nothing. His academic armor had been taken away from him, revealing him for the imposter he was.

As from a very long way away, he heard Megan's voice saying something, Megan who came from Vermont, where iced water ran naturally through the veins like Poland Spring.

"—thought you would feel that way. Because you have *principles*. I knew you would never want to stay on in a compromised position."

"What?" The red roads of Arkansas broke and fled. "Stay on?"

"Of course, you couldn't," said Megan officiously. "Not on those sorts of terms."

"Then he did offer an alternative?"

"Not one you would want to take," said Megan decidedly.

Cliff wouldn't be so sure about that. Public apologies, community service in the more plague-ridden parts of Africa, fetching Agnelli's dry cleaning for the next twelve months…. He wasn't proud. He would do any of it. "What was it?"

"Can you believe that"—Megan's mouth twisted as she groped for the appropriate invective—"that hypocrite actually told me that he'd make sure you kept your job if I *went out to dinner* with him?"

"He did what?"

"Exactly! It's disgusting! To think that you would ever want your job back on those sort of terms! To trade one infraction for another! It makes me sick!"

It made Cliff sick, too, but in quite another way.

"You told him no?" he yelped.

"Of course." Megan bristled. "What do you take me for? But he wouldn't take no for an answer, the slimy old—" When it came to theoretical jargon, Megan's vocabulary boasted a full compliment of ists and isms, but she lacked a more traditional lexicon. Shaking her head, Megan plunged on. "He wants me to write a *memo*. A memo. Can you believe it? Twenty pages justifying faculty-student hook-ups!"

"I'll write it for you," volunteered Cliff.

Megan looked at him as though he had just crawled out from under a rock. "Did you just hear what I said? He wants me to justify his hypocrisy for him—his hypocrisy with *me*!"

"It's just a dinner, right? He didn't say anything else? Just dinner?"

"He didn't specify the physical acts he wanted included, if that's what you mean. But it was highly suggested. And in a situation like this, where there is a power imbalance involved, it can never be just dinner."

"What if it were in a public place? What if you had friends sitting a table away? What if *I* sat a table away?"

"You can't really mean that. You're just pushing the parameters of the discussion."

What he was pushing was his blood pressure. Hope throbbed through his temples, relentless as a volcano about to blow.

"Please," he pleaded. "I'll never ask anything of you again. Just go to dinner with him. I'll write the memo. I'll sit there at the restaurant while you eat. I'll even walk you home, just to make sure he doesn't try anything funny. Please, just tell him yes."

Megan's face was stiff with revulsion. "What's gotten into you?"

"Desperation, that's what." He had no shame left, nothing left to hide. Just hope, painful, powerful hope. "Please. It's just until the Ad Board meeting tomorrow. Once they've decided, they've decided; he can't go back on it. You don't even have to go to dinner with him. Once the Ad Board has decided you could cop out on the bargain, say you're sick, or your schedule is all booked up, or that your mother won't let you. Whatever. He'll be too afraid someone will find out to do anything about it. It will never have to come up again. All you have to do is just say yes, just for twenty-four hours—not even twenty-four hours! Just till tomorrow morning at ten. *Please*, Megan."

"I can't believe you're asking this of me. You! Of all people! You clerked for Justice Ginsberg!"

"So have a lot of people," he snapped. He instantly realized his mistake as she took a step back. "My ideals haven't changed. I'm the still the same person. It's just the situation that's different. Megan, it's my job we're talking about—my whole career!"

"Your career? What about your principles? How can you claim to have any ideals when you're willing to betray them like this?"

"Without my job, what's the point of having ideals? What am I supposed to do, post them on a sign in the Square? Will moralize for food?"

Megan's knuckles were white on the strap of her bag. "I'm sorry I spoke for you. I'm sorry I taught for you."

"Come on, don't you think that's a bit extreme?"

"I'd sooner see the entire faculty out of a job than intercede for you!"

"Megan—"

"Ah, Megan!" Mr. Friar drowned out Cliff's *cri de coeur*. "I thought I recognized your voice. I'm so glad you decided to come by. If you don't mind waiting for me in here, I'll see Cliff out. I'll be back in just a moment."

Megan signaled her acquiescence with a stiff nod.

Placing one hand on Cliff's elbow, Friar steered the younger man towards the door.

"Did you hear that?" Cliff demanded in a hoarse whisper. "Did you hear what she said?"

"Yes." Looking grave, Friar closed the door of the OCS office behind them. "But I'm sorry you did."

"But why? Don't you see? It's my chance—if she could only be persuaded...."

"Do you really think that Arthur Agnelli would proposition a student?"

"Not usually, no. But maybe he's cracked! Maybe all those years of restraint have finally gotten to him. Megan's a good-looking girl—a bit on the austere side, but that might appeal to Professor Agnelli. It is possible!" Cliff looked anxiously at Bob Friar. "Isn't it?"

Friar just looked at him out of his clouded glasses. "Cliff," he said kindly, "if Arthur were really just after her body, why would he ask her to write him a memo?"

Cliff's mouth opened and closed again, stymied in the search for a plausible response. "Oh," he finally said. "Right. But—"

"I know Arthur," continued Friar, jabbing the down button. "He's using this as a teaching exercise. If Megan can't justify something so innocuous as a dinner with him, she certainly can't make a convincing argument for your reinstatement on the faculty."

Cliff stared fixedly at the glowing circle with its downward pointing arrow. "That does make more sense," he muttered. "But I had hoped…."

"Hope is more trouble than it's worth." The elevator pinged and the heavy doors slid open. Friar clapped Cliff on the arm, part encouragement, part prod. "Prepare your resume, and we'll talk more tomorrow. Okay?"

Looking like a bewildered child whose parents had lost him at the Zoo, Cliff obediently shuffled into the elevator. "Okay."

"Good night!" the Dean called after him, as the elevator doors closed. The last thing the Dean saw was Cliff's dazed eyes, focused on nothing in particular as he watched his life's work slide closed around him.

His own gaze calculating, the Dean contemplated the closed elevator doors. So Arthur had taken an interest in Ms. Milner? That alone wasn't enough to put the Acting Dean where he wanted him, even if he threw his own weight—carefully monitored via the machines in the gym—behind the girl's story. Most people, like Cliff, would be all too ready to believe that Arthur had intended his indecent proposal as a teaching tool.

As proposals went, it wasn't even all that indecent. Dinner might contain a multitude of meanings in the uttering, but in the repetition it shriveled into innocuousness. Students had dinner with faculty members all the time. True, it was more common to arrange such dinners in groups of two or more, but the situation was not without precedent. Megan would be excoriated for vanity or hysteria or both, while Arthur would be praised for the edginess of his pedagogical techniques and invited to keynote at the next "Classroom as Life/Life as Classroom" conference.

But there might just be another way....

Megan was prowling rather than sitting, glowering unseeingly at the bright posters on the wall like a junior Lady Macbeth. As Friar entered, she swung on one blistered heel.

"You don't believe me, do you?" she demanded. "Why would you? I almost don't believe me! Agnelli, of all people. God."

"Oh, but I do believe you." Friar regarded her shrewdly through his round glasses. "Do you have time for a little field trip?"

"Field trip?"

Grabbing up his jacket from the back of the desk chair, Friar hastily shrugged into it. "I've thought of someone who can help you out, but we'll need to go right away."

"Who is it?" Megan asked, trotting after him down the stairs.

Mr. Friar only paused long enough to hold open the back door of Pound Hall for her. "I'll tell you when we get there."

And he was off again, down the short flight of steps, up the rutted pavement of Mass Ave. Her raw heels scraping against her pumps, Megan was having a hard time keeping up. Her bag dragged on her shoulder and banged painfully against one thigh as she concentrated on putting one foot in front of the other. They passed the dress shop no one ever went to and the small huddle of building that housed Crimson Cleaners, Three Aces Pizza and Fancy Fingers, the manicure place. They passed the mellow Victorian residences that housed all-female Lesley College, the Harvard male's favorite hunting ground, conveniently positioned just behind the law school dorms. In the gray sludge of night and streetlamps, the red brick apartment buildings across the street, the small shops, the cars parked haphazardly along the narrow side streets all seemed dim and insubstantial, figments of the autumn air.

The murky peace was broken by the shrill mating call of the modern female, "Ohmigod! I'm, like, so trashed."

Across the street, the ditz brigade were out in force, simpering and squealing, clucking and clacking, clinging to the arm of any man sober enough to hold them, and some that weren't. The clatter of their stilettos on the uneven pavement sounded like a military tattoo.

Even from the other side of the street, Megan recognized Ashley K, Ashley P, and Ashley H, the

founding members of the law school sorority, the
Veritarts. Ashley K., the brains of the organization,
strutted out in front, putting her best Manolo forward
in her chosen role of Attila the Hun meets the fashion
police. Ashley K wasn't dumb; Megan had been paired
with her in a project the previous year, and found that
the quality of her written work belied the determined
inanity of her public demeanor. Nor were any of the
others (with the sole exception of Ashley P, about
whom Megan had her doubts). The phenomenon of
the Born Again Ditz bewildered Megan, but there were
too many of them at the law school to casually
discount.

Having succeeded in academics and sports,
organized charity auctions and fed the homeless in
Guatamela, the Born Again Ditz set out to achieve the
one thing she lacked: popularity. She tweaked and
plucked as assiduously as she had once studied; giggled
as though an entire African village depended on it; and
cornered the market in fashion magazines with the
same diligence with which she had once accumulated
SAT prep books. Through sheer strength of will, she
achieved a level of towering vacuity unmatched even in
Hollywood. When a perfectionist set out to become a
pea brain, she did it thoroughly and mercilessly,
scorning the unredeemed with a convert's zeal and
taking an Inquisitor's delight in casting novitiates into
the outer darkness with the damning phrase, "That is,
like, *so* last year!"

Averting her eyes, Megan hurried to catch up with
Mr. Friar. Normally, the Veritarts evoked in her
nothing but pleasurable contempt and a vague
bewilderment as to why the admissions committee
allowed them to take up good space in the classroom

and pollute the air in the Hark with their poisonous vapidity. Why go to law school, after all, when the extent of one's desiring was a large diamond on the third finger of one's left hand? They turned themselves into instruments of exploitation and set a bad example for the rest of the female population. Not to mention that they were always hogging the ellipticals at the gym.

Tonight, the swish of their tossing hair pursued Megan with a shivery whisper of kinship. Standing before Agnelli in his office, breathlessly offering up snippets of his own book back to him for his delectation, she had been no better than they. At least they were honest in their pandering. They set their own terms with the opposite sex, as much user as used. Whereas she… what had she seemed that Agnelli had thought she would agree? That breathless, that adoring, that weak?

Glancing longingly at the still-lit windows of the Starbucks across the way, Megan limped past the red and green bulk of Cambridge School of Law. Taking up a whole block, the building was shaped like an L, presumably for Law, although inebriated HLS students had been known to suggest other possibilities. For reasons known only to the architect, the longer part of the L was suspended on concrete stilts, creating a space too low to either walk or park under. Candy wrappers, cardboard Starbucks cups, and discarded textbooks littered the dark underpass. In contrast to the drab green of the façade, the shorter half of the building was constructed of bright red brick, the trailer-trash cousin of the mellow maroon of the brick buildings in the Yard. The entire edifice was coyly hedged about by red brick gateposts with "Cambridge" emblazoned on them, enabling the student body to inform the credulous that they went to school "in Cambridge," leaving their hearers to draw the obvious and erroneous conclusions.

"Are we almost there?" asked Megan, leaning against a gatepost. The upper curve of a brass C bit into her palm.

Surreptitiously, she eased her left foot out of her shoe. Her stocking clung to the back in a way that could only mean her heel had proceeded from blistering to bleeding.

"Not almost," said Mr. Friar cheerfully, indicating the glass door of Cambridge School of Law with a flourish.

"Cambridge School of Law?" said Megan dubiously, limping after him into a linoleum lined entryway that smelled of disinfectant and despair.

"Contains many unexpected treasures," countered Mr. Friar. "Wait and see."

Megan glanced gingerly around her, as if for fear her Harvard halo might tarnish from mere contact with the great un-Ivied. The cork message boards on the walls were littered with tattered posters, advertising career development classes, babysitting services, and used textbooks. Large signs on yellow paper with thick black lettering in a colloquial font reminded the student body that the deadline to sign up to take the Massachusetts Bar Exam was approaching. There used to be, Megan had been told, message boards in the tunnels beneath HLS, but those had been superceded by the large screen televisions set into the walls of the major classroom buildings.

Their classes, Megan saw, had names like *Sales & Leases* or *Wills*, terse and functional. It struck her as terribly quaint, and a little sad. It was so…vocational.

It was a far cry from the HLS catalog, where the offerings fell into a few basic categories. There was *Law and*, such as *Law and the Pursuit of Happiness*, *Law and Nineteenth Century Latin American Feminist Literature*, *Law and the Art of Motorcycle Maintenance*. Then there was the course title as postmodern statement, such as *The Ventriloquization of American Legal Thought during the Second Globalization* or *Fracture and Fragmentation: Supreme Court Jurisprudence Refracted through the Lens of a Divided Judiciary*. Finally, for the antiquarians among them, there was *Practice and Procedure in the Ancient Athenian Courts* (some knowledge of classical Greek recommended; hemlock optional) or *From Tancred to Gratian: Canon Law in the High Middle Ages* (medieval Latin and paleographic experience required).

Megan was vaguely aware that there were such things as sales and leases—and even wills—but she was profoundly grateful that she had yet to encounter any.

"Just through here," said Mr. Friar, indicating another set of glass doors, set into one side of the wall. His sweater and cords, Megan noticed, looked far less out of place in the dingy hallway than her Tahari suit. He might have been Mr. Cottar—or was Cottar the student? Megan had never seen the show, only the parodies on Saturday Night Live.

Above the glass doors, large letters spelled LIBRARY, although the Y listed drunkenly to one side. Megan would have been able to figure that out on her own, but only just. The room had little in common with the classical splendor of Langdell, with its gleaming oak tables, its patriarchal portraits, and its floor upon floor of gilt-embossed books. The Cambridge Law Library consisted of one room, as square and squat as a Cold War bomb shelter. On the ceiling, fluorescent lights had been set into the center of heavy concrete squares. The bookshelves were of the minimal metal variety, their mustard paint pocked with dirt and time. Wobbly-legged folding chairs and collapsible metal tables provided seating on either side of the room, their beige tops seamed with spilled coffee and the rainbow graffiti of indelible magic markers, where enthusiastic underlining had overshot the page. The multi-colored marks formed abstract patterns on the dingy tabletops, like confetti an hour after the parade had gone.

At the far end of the room, set between rows of pockmarked shelving, a three-sided desk demarcated the librarian's domain. It was more counter than desk, too high to sit without a stool. There was a computer on one side, with letters flashing green on a dark screen. Megan doubted one could access the internet from it. Next to it hunched a battered portable CD player, from which Tori Amos crooned, singing of disillusionment and loss.

As Megan and Mr. Friar pushed open the glass door, the woman standing behind the desk looked up, lifting her head as though the movement were an effort. Her eyes reminded Megan of a room seen through cigarette smoke.

"Can I help you?"

The fluorescent lights were as unkind to her as they were to the grimy shelves and industrial carpeting, mercilessly underscoring the sag of flesh beneath her jaw and the web of fine lines beside her eyes. Her chin length hair, straight and lusterless, was seamed with gray, and her clothes were of the variety best described as respectable. There was nothing better or worse that could be said of them. They were coverings, that was all; the means by which woman hid her nakedness having proceeded from fig leaves to the Ann Taylor sale rack. Her ensemble was, in fact, not all that different from Megan's usual choice of attire, except that her white knit shirt hung a size too large from her slumped shoulders, and her black sweater was heavy cotton rather than cashmere. Disenchantment hung about her like a disease.

Taking Megan by the arm, Friar drew her forward, still smiling gently at the woman behind the desk.

"Yes, I believe you can help us. Megan, I'd like you to meet the real author of *Legal Bodies*."

CHAPTER NINE

"Isabella: *Can this be so? Did Angelo so leave her?*

Duke: *Left her in her tears, and dried not one of them with his comfort; swallowed his vows whole, pretending in her discoveries of dishonor: in few, bestowed her on her own lamentation, which she yet wears for his sake; and he, a marble to her tears, is washed with them, but relents not.*"
— III, i, 228-234

"*We shall advise this wronged maid to stead up your appointment, go in your place. If the encounter acknowledge itself hereafter, it may compel him to her recompense: and here, by this, is your brother saved, your honor untainted, the poor Mariana advantaged, and the correct deputy scaled…. What think you of it?*"
— III, i, 254-260, 263

The color flared up into the woman's face, as harsh as a handprint. With an abrupt click, Tori Amos was

122

cut off mid-lament. The library hunched in waiting silence.

"Megan," Mr. Friar continued as easily as though they were casually communing at a cocktail party, "I'd like you to meet Marion Kucenik. She was once Arthur's graduate student."

There was a slight, but perceptible stress on the word once.

"Do I know you?" Marion crossed her arms protectively across her chest as she examined Mr. Friar's slipping toupee and oversized glasses. "Who in the hell are you?"

Mr. Friar smiled reassuringly. "My name is Bob Friar. I'm a friend of Will Arden's. And this is Megan Milner. She's a 2L at the law school." He didn't have to specify which law school. "Megan is the managing editor of the Women's Law Journal, and a member of the Board of Student Advisors. She is also about to be taken advantage of by Arthur Agnelli. Just like you."

Marion's knuckles whitened on the edge of the counter. "It wasn't like that! We were partners—a team. No one took advantage of me. Certainly not Arthur."

"No?"

"What sort of person do you take me for?" Marion drew herself up with faded dignity. "Anything I did, I chose. I'm not a doormat."

Megan tugged at the sleeves of her suit jacket. Despite the cinderblock chill of the library, the synthetic fibers of Megan's blouse clung clammily to her armpits.

"But *Legal Bodies* was your project originally, wasn't it?" Mr. Friar pressed on, never taking his eyes from Marion. "You researched it—and you wrote it."

"Authorship is a societal construct," Marion said haughtily.

"But a very potent one." Mr. Friar's voice was gentle, undemanding.

Marion seemed to wilt. "Oh, fine, maybe I did do the research." Shaking her head, she ran one jagged fingernail along a crack in the formica countertop. "It was what sent me back to the academy. I'd been working for two years in one of those big New York firms. You know the kind."

"Mm-hmm," seconded Megan emphatically, recalling her interview that afternoon.

"I originally thought of going back for a degree in Women's Studies, but I already had the legal background. And there was Arthur."

"He can be very compelling," agreed Mr. Friar.

"He's brilliant," said Marion flatly. "One of the greatest minds of our day. I heard him speak at a fundraiser for the Center for the Advancement of Women in the Legal Professions, and I knew that was where I had to be."

"It was the appropriate place for the type of work you had in mind. And a bit more than that, wasn't it?"

The restless movement of her fingernail against the countertop stopped as abruptly as the music.

"How did you know?" Marion asked jerkily. "No one was supposed to—damn."

"It's never easy to keep that sort of secret," said Mr. Friar calmingly. "Someone always sees."

"But it was so long ago!" Her face seemed to crumple along its own fault lines. "So long…."

Mr. Friar didn't say anything else. He simply waited. Megan looked from one to the other, from Bob Friar's knowing expression to Marion's bowed head, and grappled with the unthinkable. Arthur Agnelli, crusader against sexual misconduct, champion of stiffer penalties for offenders… Megan could hear his voice, harsh with authority, quoting the Regulations. *No law school faculty member shall request or accept sexual favors from or solicit a romantic or sexual relationship with any student who is enrolled in a course taught by that faculty member.* To argue that Marion Kucenik had not been in one of Agnelli's official courses would undoubtedly be, as he himself would put it, a distinction without a difference. The advisor/thesis student relationship was even more fraught with the danger of coercion than the more diffuse arena of the classroom.

"You were sleeping with Professor Agnelli?" blurted out Megan.

The librarian didn't bother to deny it. She shook her head tiredly, her eyes fixed on a past only she could see. "It was more than that. It was… a meeting of minds. We understood each other, Arthur and I."

The heavy concrete blocks of the ceiling pressed down on Megan like something out of a nightmare vision crafted by Edgar Allan Poe.

"When we spoke—it was more than a discussion. It was an act of creation. We built off each other…. I can't even explain it."

"If it was a collaboration," asked Megan, "why wasn't your name on the book? Why only his?"

"He had more clout. Oh no, not like that!" she amended hastily, in reaction to Megan's look. "He didn't pressure me into it. It was my decision as much as his. If we sent it to an academic press with my name on it, who was going to touch it? But with his, it would get the attention it deserved. And that was the point, after all, getting the message out there."

"So fewer women would be victimized," said Mr. Friar softly.

"Exactly!" Marion was as deaf to pity as she had been to betrayal. "You see, it did make sense."

"But why not be co-authors?" Megan wouldn't let go. "You'd still have all the benefit of his name, and recognition for you."

Marion devoted a great deal of concentration to a loose spar of skin on the side of her fingernail. "We didn't want to draw attention to us. To our relationship, I mean. If anyone had guessed...."

"Arthur might have been out of a job." Mr. Friar looked blandly to Megan. "The Regulations are quite clear on the subject of faculty-student relationships."

Marion worried at her nail. "That was the reason why we couldn't be seen together."

"Naturally."

"It might have gotten back to the wrong people. And Arthur didn't have tenure yet."

"It made sense for you to take every precaution."

"I took this"—Marion's despairing gesture took in the concrete walls, the pitted bookcases, the unforgiving florescence—"as an interim measure. Just until the dust settled and Arthur could maneuver a job for me at Harvard."

"And you've been here... ten years now?"

"Seven," snapped Marion.

"Of course," said Friar, so placidly that Megan suspected he had known the answer all along. "Seven."

"It's not that long."

"Of course not."

"There aren't that many jobs available."

"There never are," agreed Friar. "Especially when you haven't published."

Seven years of turning a blind eye had taken their toll; Marion didn't so much as wince at the implications. She didn't even notice them.

Diffidently, she said, "I have been working on something else—a companion piece. It's a study of the experience of women who leave law firms to go to non-profits. But it's hard. I don't have the sort of resources I had at hand when I worked with Arthur."

"What if," asked Mr. Friar softly, "I told you that you could have those resources back, and Arthur as a collaborator?"

"Has he said something? Did he send you?"

"No." Mr. Friar hastened to mitigate the effect of that abrupt negative. "But he gave an assignment to Megan that might be right up your alley."

Marion regarded Megan with a marked lack of enthusiasm. "What are you saying?" she asked flatly.

"I'm saying," said Mr. Friar persuasively, "that this gives you an ideal chance to remind Arthur just how good you were. I'm saying that you should write the paper instead of Megan."

"And then what?" asked Megan warily.

"Then," said Mr. Friar, smiling reassuringly at Megan, "we reveal the switch to Arthur—right after the Ad Board meeting."

"After Arthur speaks for Cliff?"

"Cliff?" echoed Marion blankly.

Mr. Friar put her off with a little wave of his hand. "In a moment. Well, Megan, what do you think of my little plan?"

"Let me get this straight," Megan said slowly. "We give Agnelli the memo tomorrow morning, letting him think it's from me."

"So far, so good."

"Dean Agnelli makes sure that Cliff gets off—"

"—to whatever extent he can," Mr. Friar amended. "He may have to negotiate for a year's sabbatical."

"—And then, once Cliff's case is all sewn up, we come clean."

"But only to Arthur," Mr. Friar specified, squinting thoughtfully through his dark glasses. "Not to the rest of the Ad Board."

"He will be suitably horrified and shamed—"

"Past indiscretions can do that to a man," contributed Mr. Friar cheerfully.

"—And that's the end of it."

"Not quite the end of it," said Mr. Friar, including Marion in the circle of self-satisfaction. "We inform Arthur that part of the price of our silence is citing Marion as co-author when he submits her paper to a journal. You don't mind your name coming second, do you?" he asked. "There's only so far Arthur can be pushed."

Marion shook her head dumbly.

Mr. Friar contendedly adjusted his glasses. "And so Cliff is saved, justice is served, and honor is preserved. All with just a touch of slight of hand. Neatly done, don't you think?"

"Who is Cliff?" demanded Marion.

Mr. Friar shrugged. "A minor point. Megan, if you will?"

As tersely as she could, Megan outlined the basic parameters of the situation, and the assignment Agnelli had given her. Out of consideration to the older woman's feelings, she failed to include the bit about "dinner." Hesitating only slightly, she glossed over Agnelli's advances, representing the memo itself as the sole quid pro quo for Cliff's exoneration.

She could feel Friar's approval through his grimy glasses, warming as hot apple cider.

When Megan had finished, Mr. Friar leaned confidingly forward, one elbow on the desk. "Could you write that memo up by tomorrow morning?"

For a moment, Megan caught a glimpse of the woman Marion must have been. The film had cleared from her eyes; they were alert, alive, fired with academic enthusiasm. Even the wrinkles in her forehead seemed to have smoothed out, blasted away by intellectual fervor.

"With one hand tied behind my back.

"We don't need to go quite that far," said Friar dryly. "The production of the paper is quite enough without additional acrobatics."

"It's supposed to be double-spaced, one inch margins, with pagination on the left hand corner," Megan added. "Just put my name on it—Megan Milner. That's one l, n-e-r. If you email it to me, I can email it to him, so it looks like it's coming from my email account."

"Nice touch," applauded Friar.

Megan smiled up at him, feeling the first touch of lightheartedness since the whole Cliff saga began. "Thanks."

"And if I do this, Arthur will collaborate with me again?" Marion's hands were clasped together like a schoolgirl's.

But they weren't a schoolgirl's hands. They were reddened and lined, with the veins pushing against the skin. When she had written *Legal Bodies*, they must still have been white and smooth. Like Megan's.

Megan's smile faded.

"I'll see that he does," said Mr. Friar, very gently. "We can't get you *Legal Bodies* back, not after all this time, but we can make sure you get credit for this."

With the final arrangements made, they said their farewells. In silence, they walked through the green tiled hall with its tattered posters, past the empty reception desk, out the unlocked glass doors into the still of a Cambridge night. It was late enough that the Starbucks across the street had closed, but too early still for the vast herds of migratory students who made the nightly trek from Temple Bar to Noir or Lincoln's Inn like salmon swimming upstream to mate.

Staring straight ahead of her, Megan tucked her hands into the opposing sleeves and hugged her arms close to her chest. "Ever since I came here, Professor Agnelli has been my hero. His work represented everything I wanted to do, everything I wanted to be— but he's nothing but a fraud."

In the aureole of the streetlamps, Mr. Friar's shadow stretched along beside hers down the pavement. "Surely not quite that bad. His articles, his teaching, those are still all his own. Even without *Legal Bodies*, he's still an impressive scholar in his own right. You can't deny that he has a magnificent classroom presence."

"He's no better than a thief," declared Megan bitterly, kicking at the cracks in the pavement. "He plagiarized her work!"

"It wasn't actually plagiarism as such," corrected Mr. Friar gently. "He took her basic research and some of her ideas and incorporated them into his own work. With her consent, I might add. You heard that from her own lips. It might have been unethical, but it wasn't illegal."

Dying leaves rustled overhead in mournful counterpoint. "It was still wrong—to take her work, her ideas...."

"How is that any different from the work of a research assistant, or a judicial clerk? Most of the opinions in your casebooks weren't written by the judges whose names they bear. And yet no one raises an eyebrow about that."

"But in that case it's understood, it's part of the original deal," Megan struggled with inchoate notions of fairness, groping for half-remembered classroom jargon. Even the foggiest idea could sound official if one clapped a legal tag on it. "It's like a work for hire. At least they go in *knowing.* You can't really believe it's the same."

"No. I don't. But that's how Arthur, I'm sure, must have justified it to himself. Although even he would have to admit that the romantic relationship rather complicated matters."

"He used her affection to suck her mentally dry. And then he dropped her."

"He wouldn't view it that way."

They walked in silence for a few moments, down the deserted length of Mass Ave, past the silent apartment buildings and crooked side streets and the stores that closed by nine.

As they passed the placid old Victorians that housed Lesley College, Friar said thoughtfully, almost to himself, "Arthur reacts more strongly to ideas than people. He always has. While the strength of the intellectual attraction lasted, I'm sure he genuinely believed he cared for her. At least," amended Friar, with a wry, sidelong glance, "he wanted her, and in our society that serves as much the same thing. Once the idea had been exhausted, so was the attraction. He lost interest."

"That's just putting a different wrapper on the same thing," objected Megan, who had little interest in the analysis of human nature, and less in subtleties. "He still used her and dropped her."

"But he didn't see it that way. If you award any significance to intent, he is innocent of that much."

Megan scuffed moodily at a fallen leaf, but refrained from comment.

"And she was right, too," Mr. Friar continued conversationally. "The book would never have been nearly as well received had it come from her. I've heard it hailed as a *Feminine Mystique* for the legal profession. It has, I am told, made a real difference in the lives of a number of female lawyers."

"It made a difference to me," said Megan, almost inaudibly. "It's why I chose to go to law school."

"There you have it. The good of the many or one woman's career? It all depends on which way you go about looking at the situation."

By mutual consent, they paused on the corner of Everett Street, in front of the pastel windows of the dress shop no one ever entered. Megan tucked her hands into her sleeves and looked up at Mr. Friar with a wrinkle between her neatly plucked brows.

"That's not a fair dichotomy. Not when the situation should never have happened in the first place."

"Which is why we're not going to let it happen again. See you tomorrow morning?"

"In the third floor lounge of Griswold," Megan parroted obediently.

"That's my girl." Friar patted her bracingly on the shoulder.

Megan knew she ought to take umbrage at being called girl, but she was too tired and too confused to quibble, and there was something very comforting about Bob Friar's assertiveness, no matter how he chose to express it.

"Don't worry," he said. "We'll get this sorted out yet."

The Dean was feeling quite pleased with himself as he cut across Mass Ave. He admired Arthur, he always had, but all that rampant saintliness was a bit much to live with. It was very hard having an old Testament prophet constantly at one's office door, thundering of doom and demanding retribution, like a cranky Moses with a much longer set of commandments, beginning with "thou shalt not use a gender specific pronoun," and going rapidly downhill from there. At least with the stone tablets, once one broke, it was gone. With computer printouts, Arthur could paper his office indefinitely.

The Dean breathed in a satisfied lungful of crisp September air. After tonight, he had Arthur just where he wanted him. Still at the university, still turning out brilliant—if incomprehensible—articles filled with the jargon for which he was so justly famous, still raising money and running conferences and gathering a good-sized crowd to his annual lecture class on feminist legal theory, but out of moral capital, out of the Dean's office and out of his hair. How could a man with a history of sexual misconduct lobby for stricter school guidelines? His nose would grow every time he pressed the print button on another ream of those tedious draft regulations.

Oh, yes, it was a happy, happy day for the Dean, the law school, and for trees everywhere.

The trees of Cambridge Common nodded to the Dean in acknowledgment, tacitly thanking him for his intervention on behalf of their pulpy fellows. Just across the street from the law school, Cambridge Common provided a patch of calm in the middle of campus, a nod to calmer, greener days when the law school was barely a glint in an educator's eye, and the cobbled streets were little more than cow paths. There were quicker way to get from the law school to the Dean's well-tended Victorian house on Brattle Street, but none that evoked the same sensations of satisfaction.

Cutting across the green, in the towering white shadow of the Civil War monument, the Dean always felt a pleasant sense of timelessness, a kinship with the men who had walked here before. George Washington had mustered troops here, in the desperate days of the Revolution. Oliver Wendell Holmes must have wandered and mused beneath the shade of some of those same leafy trees, composing those scathing sentences which so delighted the Dean in his days as a young law student. Here radicals had raised their placards, and Radcliffe girls had lowered their morals. The green grass and the red brick walls and the wind among the tree branches whispered to the Dean of the life of the academy, of Washington and Holmes, Christopher Columbus Langdell and Archibald Cox, jurists and judges, philologists and philosophers, poets and patriots, girls in bobby sox and boys in beanies, all woven together in the same irregular tapestry of time and place. And he, himself, there with them, in the shadowy fellowship of a September night.

There was someone else there, though. The Dean heard them before he saw them, shambling footsteps and slurred voices, like something out of a horror movie or a college frat party. In this case, it was decidedly the latter. Two boys in baggy jeans and baseball caps zig-zagged across the Dean's path. The diagonal was by accident rather than design; linked at the shoulders like a two-headed Caliban, neither seemed to have much control of the steering. Peaceful, the Common might generally be, but it lay just to the south of Follen Street, where an innocuous white frame house housed Lincoln's Inn and enough alcohol to permanently incapacitate an entire troupe of elephants.

The Dean drew back, out of the way of the drunken duo, but it was too late. In slow motion, he watched as the stockier of the two uncurled his arm from about the others neck, jack-knifed forward, and spewed out a chunky mass of noxious substance with a vigor that put Old Faithful to shame.

"Shit, Paul!" ejaculated his companion.

It was, in fact, another substance entirely. And it was all over the Dean's hand sewn Italian leather loafers.

"Sorry 'bout that!" The baseball cap wearing wonder clapped the Dean heartily on the arm, sloshing beer across the Dean's feet. "Paul, here, he can't hold his liquor. Nada tolerance. Zero. Zippo. Niente."

Glumly contemplating the wreck of his shoes, the Dean extracted a linen handkerchief from his breast pocket—just because he was in disguise didn't mean one had to forego the amenities of a gentleman—and broke into the recitation of negatives.

"Here," the Dean said flatly. "Wipe his face."

Another retching noise came from the ground.

"When he's done," the Dean added, as a precaution.

"Heeeeeeey!" exclaimed baseball cap boy, entirely ignoring his suffering friend. "You're the new OCS guy! Yeah!"

"Yeah," agreed the Dean, who had always prided himself on his ability to master local dialects. It was one of the talents that made him so effective as a fundraiser. There was nothing like being asked for money in one's own idiom.

"Let me tell you," confided Baseball Cap, staggering a bit on a fallen twig, "you came at the wrong time. The wroooooong time. This school has been a fucking mess since the Dean left. A super fucking mess."

"Really?" One did like one's absence to be appreciated, even if it was by such a creature as this.

"Yeah." Baseball Cap shook his head sadly. "Old Agony, he's a fucking robot."

"Robots…" echoed the boy on the ground, before subsiding again into heaves, although whether he were seconding the character assessment or contemplating the manifold wonders of mechanization was unclear.

Baseball Cap ignored him. "He doesn't understand that a guy's gotta do what a guy's gotta do. Now the old Dean… there was a dude."

"Hmm." The Dean wasn't quite sure what was meant by that, but it sounded suitably complimentary. "How so?"

"Just a dude, y'know? A guy's guy. A man's man."

The Dean made a note to advise the Admissions Office to add a basic literacy test as part of the admissions process.

Swaying on his feet, Baseball Cap warmed to his topic. "He wouldn't kick someone out just for scamming on a student, not the old Dean. He could've taught us all a thing or two. Yeah. *He* wasn't a fucking glacier."

"Gah," said Paul and subsided into his own vomit.

"Don't you think you should help your friend?" inquired the Dean frostily.

Baseball Cap gestured expansively with his beer bottle. "Oh, I could tell you a thing or two about the old Dean...."

"Could you?" said the Dean grimly.

"Oh, yeah." Baseball Cap swung an arm around the Dean's shoulder, fanning his face with warm beer. "Like, for starters, why do you think his wife divorced him? Hunh?"

Five years on, his divorce was still a sensitive topic. The Dean shrugged out from under Baseball Cap's arm. "Did you ever consider that it might have been the other way around?"

"Whaaa? You're pulling my leg, right?" That wasn't all the Dean would have liked to pull. "Nah, it's because she *found out.* About all the other women."

The Dean only wished. A law school didn't just run itself. Between fundraisers and faculty meetings, he hadn't had time for one woman, much less many. His mistress, if one chose to view it that way, had been HLS. He hadn't been on a date since... well, since Ann. It was a depressing recollection.

"You know that building on Chauncy Street?" Baseball Cap was on a roll. His friend, meanwhile, appeared to have passed out. "The one with all the balconies? That's where he meets them. I know 'cause I have a friend with a place there, and he said that he knew someone who saw the Dean there. In his tighty-whities."

"And nothing else?" enquired the Dean, who wore boxers. "That sounds a bit chilly."

Baseball Cap dismissed inconsistencies with a shrug of his shoulders. "He must've got locked out. Or something like that."

"Something," said the Dean, who had never, to his knowledge entered any apartment building on Chauncy Street, clothed or otherwise. "Have you ever stopped to ponder that your friend's friend might have been misinformed? It might be wise to think twice before you spread rumors. Completely *unfounded* rumors."

Baseball Cap regarded him pityingly.

"You just don't know the old Dean like I do. We're like…" Baseball Cap held up two fingers and made a concerted effort to cross them, crossing his eyes in the process. "Like *this*."

"Indeed."

"The old Dean, he looked out for his bros…." Baseball Cap shook his head in fond recollection. "Like 1L year, our Civ Pro exam, some of us got hold of the exam questions before the exam, y'know what I mean? Not like cheating, just like, *anticipating*. Agnelli would've come down us like a ton of fucking bricks, but the Old Dean, he just called us in, asked us a few questions, and let us go. Just like that. Sweet."

"Sweet, indeed," echoed the Dean.

At least for those who had gotten away with it. He really ought to go about in disguise more often; one learned such interesting things. The Dean filed the information away for future reference.

He vaguely remembered that case. There had been allegations that ten members of the 1L class—ten members who were, coincidentally, all now on the Law Review—had cheated on their Civil Procedure exam. The professor was known to reuse old exams; it saved him the trouble of writing new ones. He recycled them on a five year schedule, occasionally changing the names of the characters in the hypotheticals when he remembered to get around to it, but otherwise leaving them just as they were. It wasn't all that hard to track down copies of the old exams, but, for the most part, an honor system prevailed.

Last January, whispers of malfeasance had made their way to the Dean's office. No one claimed that the boys had plagiarized, merely that they had written their own answers ahead of time, with the unfair advantage of leisure. It would have been all too easy. With exams all taken on personal laptops, all the boys had to do was open a pre-prepared file and paste the contents into a new file created at the appropriate time. Then they could sit back and twiddle their thumbs for three and a half hours while their colleagues desperately raced against time to produce answers to the four complicated sets of problems.

But the boys had all sworn right and left that they had produced their answers within the allotted examination time. They produced outlines and study guides, all heavily underlined and annotated, as evidence of their diligence in studying. Short of taking apart their hard drives to try to find evidence of expunged files or doctored dates, there had been nothing else that could be done.

Besides, an investigation might have led to a scandal, and a scandal might have driven down their US News & World Report ratings. Applications would have dropped, donations gone down.... What was a little potential cheating compared with a problem like that?

It had been far easier to take the boys at their word and let the whole incident go.

"I might be seeing Dean Arden pretty soon," the Dean said cunningly. "And since you two are so close, I'm sure he'll want to hear about all the glowing things you said about him. Who should I say was speaking?"

Baseball Cap puffed out his chest. "Gabe Lucas. He'll know who I am."

"Now he will."

Smiling a crocodile smile, the Dean waved and strode away across the Common.

"Far better than you knew him."

CHAPTER TEN

"Duke: *And here comes Claudio's pardon*....
This is the pardon, purchased by such sin,
For which the pardoner himself is in....
Pray you, let's hear.

Provost [reads the letter]: Whatsoever you may hear of the
contrary, let Claudio be executed by four of the clock.... Thus fail
not to do your office as you will answer for it at your peril."
  -- IV, ii, 103, 110-111, 121-129

"Isabella: *Hath yet the deputy sent my brother's pardon?*

Duke: *He hath released him, Isabel, from the world;*
His head is off, and sent to Angelo.

Isabella: *O, I will to him and pluck out his eyes!*

Duke: ... *If you can, pace your wisdom*
In that good path that I would wish it to go,

And you shall have your bosom on this wretch,
Grace of the Duke, revenges to your heart,
And general honor.

Isabella: *I am directed by you.*"
  -- IV, iii, 115-117, 121, 134-138

In the third floor lounge of Griswold Hall, the more conscientious members of the Ad Board were already beginning to gather. The Provost did not fall into the category of the conscientious, but he did like to make sure he got his coffee, and the line at the small machine preceding a meeting was frequently prohibitive. Ever since suffering through an extended two hour wrangle about budgeting without a hot beverage, the Provost had made it a policy to arrive at any faculty meetings at least ten minutes early. Among other things, sometimes catering provided cookies and those excellent chocolate brownies cut into triangles. The Provost was really quite fond of the brownies, even though, as a brownie purist, he believed that they ought to be eaten in rectangles, as God and Betty Crocker intended.

The Provost cast a jealous glance at the coffee machine, but so far his only competition was a tall man with a mop of unruly black hair, dressed in clothes that brought back painful memories of the Provost's younger days. The platform shoes had given him fallen arches—and without them, his bell bottoms just wouldn't fall right. It was one of those memories he did his best to suppress, along with all pictures from his college years.

"Hi," he said, sidling up to the newcomer and sticking out his hand, partially out of hospitality, but largely to establish his status as next in line for the coffee machine. "Charles Epstein. I'm the Provost. And you are…."

"Bob Friar." The Dean added a bit of a Southern drawl, just in case Chaz recognized his voice. It didn't matter that the Dean had never been South of the Mason-Dixon line for longer than the length of a conference. Chaz was from Westchester; he wouldn't know a steel magnolia from a Georgia peach. "I'm the new OCS hire."

"Nice to meet you, nice to meet you." The Dean need not have worried. Having performed the necessary amenities and established his place in line, the Provost's attention was absorbed by the pre-packaged cups of Green Mountain coffee set out for the benefit of the faculty. "Have you seen the decaf Hazelnut Crème?" he asked, peering myopically at the cardboard dispensers.

"Here." The Dean handed him a plastic cup from the appropriately marked box. "In the decaf Hazelnut Crème box."

"Fancy that," marveled the Provost, fumbling the little cup into the machine. "How unusual."

"Are you here for the Ad Board meeting?" prodded the Dean as the Provost jabbed the brew button.

"What's that? Oh, yes. How did you hear about it?"

The Dean shrugged, as the machine grunted and burbled. Coffee gurgled grudgingly into the Provost's cup. "Who hasn't?"

The Provost sighed. "True enough. It's a bad situation all around. Poor Cliff."

"Why poor Cliff?"

"I suppose you could look at it that way," mused the Provost as he reached for his cup. "Which of us wouldn't like an excuse to get away from these Cambridge winters, eh?"

"I'm sorry," said the Dean slowly. "I'm afraid you've lost me. I'd heard that the Acting Dean had changed his mind. And if Arthur Agnelli puts his weight behind Cliff...."

"I don't know who you've been talking to, but they must be nuts. Arthur change his mind? Not on this green earth."

The Dean moved automatically aside to allow the Provost access to the refrigerator tucked away beneath the counter. "It's more orange and brown at present. Perhaps you just haven't heard yet."

"No such luck. Arthur sent a note this morning indicating that it was all systems go, full speed ahead. Bye-bye, Cliff."

"You mean he sent a note last night?" The Dean was so alarmed that he completely forgot to be Southern. Fortunately, the Provost, immersed in the intricacies of beverage production, failed to notice.

"Noooo." The Provost added a miserly drop of cream to his coffee, frowned, and poured in a generous splash. Diets, after all, were for junior faculty. "Just an hour ago. I don't know why he bothered. It wasn't as though he hadn't made himself clear before."

"Mm-hmm," said the Dean.

"I don't know where we're going to find another lecturer on such short notice. But that's just like Arthur Agnelli. I wish, just once, he would stop to consider the practicalities before he gets on his high horse." The Provost sighed and shook his head. "I suppose we could try to get one of the other lecturers to take on an extra section, but they get so snippy about that sort of thing. We can't just combine two sections, because then the students will get snippy. And if we throw money at the problem and hire someone away from another law school, the trustees will get snippy. And they'll all come complaining to me. There's just no winning. Are you all right?" added the Provost, belatedly noting his companion's silence. "You're looking a bit green around the gills."

"Just a touch of indigestion," managed Friar, with an unconvincing smile.

The Provost peered nervously into his cup. "I hope it isn't the coffee. My acid reflux—"

"Will you excuse me for a moment? I just remembered something I forgot to do."

"Of course!" Still distractedly tilting the contents of his cup, the Provost flapped a hand in farewell. "Nice talking to you. Feel better!"

Easing his cell phone out of his pocket, the Dean hurried into the stairwell and punched in a well-known number.

"Hello?" said a distracted voice. In the background, the Dean could hear the slow swish of liquid.

"Chaz? It's me." The Dean moved a bit further into the stairwell as a precaution against tell-tale echoes.

"Will?" The swishing abruptly stopped. "I can't tell you how much we've missed you! It's been a nightmare. Agnelli's coming down on everyone like a ton of bricks. That lecturer affair—"

"I know, I know. I heard. Look, I've changed my plans. I should be back sometime today."

"Hallelujah!"

The Dean cut the Provost off before he could go into a round of *Ride the Chariot*. When the spirit moved him, Chaz managed a truly alarming descant. "Can you do me a favor?"

"Anything. Well, almost anything. It depends on what it is."

The Dean knew his old friend well. "Don't worry, Chaz, it won't interfere with your massage. I just need you to delay the Ad Board meeting for me."

There was a pause on the other end, followed by the Provost's reluctant voice, slower than a student in January. "I dunno, Will. Arthur is pretty hard to delay. It's like standing in front of a locomotive."

"I'll make sure you don't get run over," promised the Dean, shaking back his sleeve to check his watch. "You don't have to do anything dramatic. Just delay. Say you forgot your report and have to go back to the office to get it. Say you were called out on an important call. Hide Arthur's favorite pen. Hit the fire alarm. I don't care how you do it, just so long as you make sure the meeting doesn't start before I can get there, understand?"

"I'll try."

"Don't try. Do."

"Okay." The Provost still sounded dubious. "You won't be long, will you?"

"That depends on how long I stand here talking to you," muttered the Dean.

"Huh? What was that?"

"No, Chaz, I won't be long. Ciao."

Snapping his phone shut, the Dean scowled at the banister, making a concerted effort to contain his irritation. Giving way to pique wouldn't solve anything. Damn! He had badly misjudged. He had been so sure that once having put his proposition to Megan, Arthur would follow through on his half of the deal—and, having once followed through, would be vulnerable to a little friendly coercion. Cliff would be redeemed, by Arthur's hand rather than his own, and he would then, in turn, be able to lean on Arthur. All neat and tidy— and entirely irredeemable.

One would think, having known Arthur all this time, he could have called it better. And he called himself a student of human nature! There he had been, smugly explaining Arthur to Megan the night before, his way of conflating intellect and desire, of pushing aside anything he didn't want to see. Arthur sure as hell wouldn't want to see Cliff after propositioning Megan. It all followed as night did the day, and the Dean had been a fool not to see it.

The Dean tapped the edge of his phone impatiently against the banister, trolling for inspiration, so many clicks to the thought. They still had Marion; they still had the memo. If Arthur could be shocked into an admission of guilt….

Someone bumped into the Dean on a beeline for the third floor lounge. Automatically, the Dean caught the girl before she tripped, and found himself holding Megan by the shoulders, cashmere soft as memory beneath his fingers. The scent of shampoo rose from her hair like incense, underpinned by the muskier odor of spilled coffee.

Releasing her, the Dean took a rapid step back, automatically lifting a hand to make sure his wig was properly in place.

Megan shook back her hair, tipping her head back to look up at him with eyes ringed with dark smudges of sleeplessness.

"Have they started yet? Is there any word?"

"There is. But it's not good."

"What do you mean not good?"

"I mean that the Acting Dean doesn't seem to have changed his tune regarding Cliff."

"I don't understand. I sent the memo, just the way we planned. I know it reached him, because he emailed me back, saying he would expect to see me this evening. For *dinner*." Megan's lips twisted as if the word left a sour taste in her mouth.

Friar looked grim. "Well, he reneged."

"That bastard!" exploded Megan. "If he thinks— I'll arrange a sit in. I'll picket his office. I'll call every paper in the metro Boston area. I'll—"

"Whoa, there!" Friar held up a hand to stem the flood of anti-Agnelli initiatives. "Not so fast. We can redeem this situation yet."

"But how? If he's not keeping his end of the bargain, I don't see what we can do, other than go public with everything."

"Ah, that's because you don't know what I know." Friar grinned at her, a high-spirited, daredevil grin that acted on Megan's frazzled nerves like Red Bull. Either that, or the triple espresso she had gulped to get her through her morning class was finally kicking in.

"What?" she demanded.

"The Dean—the real Dean—is returning. Today. This morning!"

"But what if he doesn't believe us?"

"Oh, he'll believe us. We'll make sure he believes us. Do you trust me?"

Megan looked at him hopelessly. "What other choice do I have?"

"Not exactly flattering, but it will do. Here's the plan. The Dean is due to arrive within the next fifteen minutes, just in time for the Ad Board meeting. I want you to get there right then, before Agnelli has the chance to give the Dean his version of events. Good so far?"

Megan nodded.

"I want you to confront him as though *you* wrote the memo—not Marion."

"But—"

"Arthur thinks you wrote it. It will be more complicated if you have to explain away an extra layer of confusion. Not to mention that it will be more moving coming from a student rather than a middle-aged librarian. It makes the transgression seem greater."

"I suppose," Megan said reluctantly. "But I still don't see why the Dean should believe me, unless Agnelli confesses. I'm still nothing but a hysterical student."

"You underrate yourself. Don't worry, I've considered that. There'll be back-up on hand, in the form of Marion, and I have a few aces of my own hidden up my sleeve. Unfortunately," he added, "I can't be here myself."

"Why not?" Megan felt absurdly betrayed. Of course, it was nonsense, she was perfectly capable of managing on her own, and she did have a legitimate grievance to propound, but she still felt like a toddler whose security blanket had been brutally wrenched away just before the first day of nursery school.

"OCS business," Friar said. "And I'm late already."

Megan glanced dispiritedly at the corridor that led to the lounge. "I'll let you know how it goes."

"Courage!" Taking her hand, Friar squeezed it lightly. "Remember, the owl of Minerva only flies after the dust has settled."

"And that means…."

Friar paused halfway down the flight of stairs to glance back up at her. In the dim light of the stairwell, the exuberant wig shielded his face as effectively as John Wayne's cowboy hat. "That no matter how chaotic things may seem over the next few hours, everything will turn out just fine."

He was gone around the bend before Megan could ask by what right he sounded quite so sure.

With an irritable sigh, Megan reached into her bag for a notebook and began to outline her opening oration. So much for Bob Friar and all his schemes. So much for idiot Gabe, who had gotten her into this in the first place. So much for men.

She and Minerva were on their own.

CHAPTER ELEVEN

"This deed unshapes me quite ….
Alack, when once our grace we have forgot,
Nothing goes right; we would, and we would not."
    -- IV, iv, 22, 33-34

Out of habit, Agnelli had gone first to his former office.

With the portfolio containing his notes on the Cliff Walker case under his arm, he descended the broad marble stairs of Hauser Hall into the white-walled basement. Ahead of him lay computer services, a handful of computers and a help desk staffed by the more technologically inclined sort of law student. Although the undergraduate computer science center was only yards away, situated in the Science Center in the no-man's land between the law school and the Yard, the law school preferred to keep its own internal services, just as it did with the tiny doctor's office tucked away in an odd corner of basement beneath Pound Hall. Like a feudal fief, the law school contained a host of amenities within the boundaries of its own demesne: computer help, health services, copy center, and a number of mysterious offices whose function no one knew except the people who worked in them, an entire world contained within the basement of the law school.

Agnelli turned left, passing the rows of brightly colored lockers that made the basement look more like a high school than an institution of higher learning. A class period must have just let out, because the tunnels bustled like a brightly colored anthill. All around him, students were heaving heavy textbooks off the upper shelves of their lockers, exchanging bookbags for gym bags, and greedily draining the last dregs from the beige and brown Styrofoam cups that catering services provided for their free coffee. Some lucky few had stopped at Starbucks before class, and proudly carried cups blazoned with their distinctive green logo. The artier among them boasted the distinctive orange cups of Toscanini's, the coffee shop in the Square manned by a staff who were all pierced, tattooed or dreadlocked, and sometimes all three. People bustled up and down the hall, weaving around their fellows, spilling coffee on themselves, and calling out breathless greetings.

Signs on the wall directed the directionless towards the various buildings served by the tunnels. Agnelli took the southerly route towards Griswold, passing a large bulletin board hung with forgotten fliers, one of the last to remain in the law school's new digitized age. The rest of the hallway was dotted with a series of innocuous art prints, chosen by a long-forgotten functionary. At least, they had been intended as innocuous. To Agnelli, they all spoke of a shameful chauvinist past, from the poster advertising a history of shoes at the Metropolitan Museum's Costume Institute, tottery, improbable things, designed to impede a woman's movement, to old movie fliers trumpeting the performances of Jimmy Stewart and Kim Novaks— movies that, no doubt, only served to reaffirm the normative paradigm of traditional gender roles, indoctrinating generations of women into unquestioning servitude.

At the bend of the hallway, just before the entrance to Langdell North, a faceless woman in red danced with a dark suited man on a rainy street-corner. Agnelli's well trained mind overlooked the incongruity of dancing in the deluge, and automatically noted the confluence of the color of shame—from the Bible through Hester Prynne—and the lack of a face. It was a brilliant allegory of dancing as a coercive act, in which the man, "leading," steered the woman out of the bounds of polite society, thus "shaming" and stigmatizing her, as exemplified by the scarlet dress.

At some point, once the Cliff Walker affair was dealt with, he really would have to speak to someone about changing the decorating scheme in the basement. The young minds of America's elite were so impressionable, so easily led astray.

Agnelli took a sharp right, past a battered vending machine, into the narrow doorway that led into the stairwell of Griswold Hall. Upstairs, the members of the Ad Board would be gathering, preparatory to deciding Cliff Walker's fate. Not that there was much deciding left to do. He had made his feelings on that quite clear. Cliff had to go. He had broken the rules.

It didn't change anything that Megan's memo had been good. Very good.

It had been in his inbox when he woke at his usual hour of five, coming neatly awake without the aid of an alarm. It was still there when he came back from his daily jog along the seedier byways of Central Square (consciousness-raising being infinitely preferable to the insipid postcard prettiness of the Charles River), still with the same stiff introductory note: "Dear Professor Agnelli, Please find attached the document you requested. Yours, Megan Milner." Brusque, but a capitulation nonetheless. Agnelli respected the terseness of it; he had fought enough battles in his time to know that the worthiest adversaries seldom accepted surrender graciously.

It was exactly as he had specified, twenty pages, double spaced, with one inch margins and pagination on the lower left hand corner, written with an economy of style that elicited several approving nods, the most effusive encomium in the Acting Dean's lexicon. Economy of style, but what breadth of reference, what scope of ideas! It was astounding that a girl in her twenties should have read so widely or so well, or achieved such a deeply nuanced synthesis of the various stages in the women's movement.

He hadn't seen work of that caliber since.... Well, for a very long time.

In fact, the very excellence of the memo was all the more reason for Cliff to go. If he pardoned Cliff, he would be guilty of taking part in a meretricious bargain. If he, however, refused to complete the trade—well, then, the corrupt exchange had never happened. His hands were clean.

At least, they were clean on the outside, and that was all anyone could see. The spots on his soul were his own concern, and his alone.

"Agnelli!" In the Griswold lounge, the Provost hailed him with a raised cup of coffee. "Guess what? Excellent news! Arden is coming back!"

Agnelli's fingers tightened convulsively on the portfolio under his arm. "When?"

"Today!" The Provost practically capered in his enthusiasm. His rubicund face was flushed with pleasure and just a tiny bit of malice. The Provost and Agnelli had never coexisted comfortably. They were Athens and Sparta, Cavalier and Roundhead, Oscar and Felix. Agnelli had no doubt that, internally, Epstein was singing a rousing chorus of "Ding, Dong, the Witch is Dead," complete with dancing munchkins. "Isn't it great! He just called—he must have been on his way back from the airport."

"This must certainly bring great pleasure to everyone who knows him," said Agnelli gravely, helping himself to a plastic packet of coffee. No Hazelnut Crème or Swiss Chocolate Almond for Agnelli; he took his coffee plain and black. The movement helped to hide the slight trembling of his hands.

There was no need for tremors. She wouldn't say anything. She would be a fool to say anything. Even if she did speak, his reputation was such that any allegation would redound on her, tainting her with the tarnish meant for him. With Cliff safely expunged from the faculty, there would be nothing left to reproach him, nothing that could come back to threaten him.

He was safe. Just as he had been the last time.

Or, at least, he would be safe, as soon as Cliff's hearing was over and done with. The more expeditiously it was conducted, the better.

"Must be a load off for you, eh, Agnelli?" The Provost beamed cherubically. "Looking forward to returning to civilian life?"

Agnelli neatly pushed the brew button, employing exactly the necessary amount of pressure. "I hope I will always endeavor to rise to whatever challenge is given to me."

"Mmph," said the Provost.

"And I would feel remiss in my duties if I abandoned my work mid-task, simply because someone else will soon be here to take up the reins. Since the Advisory Board is already assembled, I suggest that we carry on with this matter of Cliff Walker. We don't want to be boring Will with it when he comes back."

"What don't you want to bore me with?"

The Dean strode into the room, resplendent in gray wool and a maroon tie that made the other men's attire look like last year's sample sale. A crackle of energy entered the room with him, an effortless air of authority that he carried with him as easily as his monogrammed cufflinks.

"Will!" The Provost greeted him with a cry of relief. "I can't tell you how glad I am that you're back."

"Don't even try," said the Dean, clapping his old friend on the back. "I wouldn't want you to strain something."

"You," said the Provost reproachfully, "just don't understand what it is to have a delicate constitution."

"And I praise God for it daily. Arthur!" No slaps on the back for the Acting Dean. Such a gesture would be an act of lese majesty akin to high-fiving a plaster saint. The Dean greeted Agnelli with outspread arms, and was received in turn with a stiff nod of greeting. "My other self! How do you like being Dean?"

"I don't envy you the paperwork," Agnelli said dryly, removing his cup from the machine.

"So true, so true," mourned the Dean, shaking his head. "It's not nearly as glamorous a job as it looks, is it? But you've done wonders, Arthur! And in only a week! You wouldn't believe the reports I've heard of you. As always, you have exceeded all my expectations."

Agnelli snapped a plastic lid onto his coffee cup. "I had thought you intended to be away longer."

"Don't let that worry you! My business was concluded more expeditiously than I had expected."

"How fortunate for all of us." Agnelli's expression was everything that was correct and unenthusiastic.

"Now, what's been going on in that fertile mind of yours since I've been gone? New articles, new initiatives, new directions for your Women's Center? Don't tell me that you haven't been brewing something. I know you far too well for that."

Under the Dean's practiced familiarity, Agnelli thawed visibly. "It is true. I have begun working on a new project."

"Really?" The Dean availed himself of Agnelli's elbow and began steering him across the lounge. "Tell me more."

"The topic was brought to my attention by the sorry affair of that young lecturer."

"Ah, student-faculty relationships! Topical, Arthur, very topical. But, then, you always were excellent at capturing a trend."

"I'm hoping to get an article out of it; perhaps a longer work, if the material calls for it."

"Oh, I think you'll be surprised just what it will stretch to," said the Dean merrily. "All sorts of unexpected avenues…. Here, now! What's this?"

A slim figure in black had slipped in front of them, barring their progress to the Dean's office.

Now that the moment had arrived, Megan felt her confidence deserting her, along with the remnants of her former coffee buzz. Appealing to the Dean had seemed quite easy in the abstract, but it was different when he was standing right in front of her, brisk and business-like in a perfectly tailored suit and a tie that was a shade too dark to officially be called a power tie. He exuded authority like an electric fence.

Nor had Megan expected to see him quite so chummy with his temporary successor. Of course, she had known that they had been on the faculty together for quite some time, but the faculty was large and their spheres were as far apart as the sun and the moon. Dean Arden, when he taught, taught Corporations, with the occasional seminar on advanced topics in Corporate Governance. Professor Agnelli, on the other hand, in addition to his expertise in Feminist Legal Theory taught the required Legal Professions class (with emphasis on the changing status of women and minorities), International Human Rights, and a seminar called Rebellious Lawyering that addressed such topics as the basics of picketing, consciousness-raising groups, and lobbying. They had nothing in common.

The familiarity of Dean Arden's hand on Professor Agnelli's elbow said otherwise. Megan caught herself nervously fiddling the with the bottom button on her cashmere sweater and made herself stop. It was those sorts of gestures that were a dead giveaway. People took you seriously when you behaved like someone to be reckoned with—at least, so said chapter twenty-two of *Legal Bodies*.

Remembering the wasted form of *Legal Bodies*' legitimate author, Megan drew herself up assertively.

"Please excuse my barging in on you like this, Dean Arden," she said briskly. "But if I might trouble you for a moment of your time?"

The Dean favored her with a politician's smile, empty air clothed in compassion. "You can have more than a moment, but at a more opportune time. As you can see, we're just on our way into a meeting. And there should be a few others joining us…." The Dean looked quizzically at the Provost.

"They're on their way," the Provost said, squinting madly in a clumsy attempt at a wink. "They said to tell you they'd be fifteen minutes late."

"What, all of them?" asked the Dean mildly. His smile broadened as the Provost made a series of indecipherable gestures designed to be subtle. "It's all right, Chaz, don't go into convulsions on me."

Sensing she was losing her moment—if she had ever had a moment—Megan stepped boldly forward, forcing the Dean to acknowledge her presence.

"I think you'll want to hear this before you have your meeting. It involves a grave breech of school policy—by someone who ought to have known better."

Under Agnelli's signature shock of hair, his eyes were as unreadable as the onyx orbs of an archaic idol. He might have been carved out of stone.

"Well, that does sound intriguing! I'll never be able to sit through a meeting with that sort of suspense hanging over me," the Dean said jocularly. "And we do have fifteen minutes, it seems.... But Arthur is still Acting Dean here. He'll hear you out, won't you, Arthur?"

Megan took a deep breath. "It's a basic principle that no man can be judge in his own case. Which is why I'm appealing to you, Dean Arden, rather than the Acting Dean."

An expression of deep confusion spread across the Dean's distinguished face. "Are you saying that Arthur...?"

"Yes," Megan said fiercely, and pressed her lips very tightly together at the end of the word, as if for fear it might be taken from her otherwise.

"What infraction could Arthur possibly have committed? The idea of Arthur misbehaving... the mind boggles." The Dean glanced at the two other faculty members, inviting them to share the joke. "Professor Agnelli is HLS's best advertisement for the straight and narrow, aren't you, Arthur?"

"I do my best," Agnelli said stiffly.

"If best can be defined as serving his own interests at the expense of others." Once started, there was no turning back. "What would you say if I told you that Professor Agnelli had abused his position to proposition a student? What would you say if I told you that he tried to trade extracurricular favors for the exercise of his academic office?"

"The girl is clearly overwrought," said Agnelli. "She doesn't know what she's saying."

The Dean patted his arm in an unspoken gesture of reassurance.

To Megan, he said, not unkindly, "I would say that you have been working too hard. HLS can be a stressful place, even for our very best and brightest.

Sometimes, when you're tired and frazzled, all sorts of things seem plausible. If you go to University Health Services, they have a number of excellent Mental Health practitioners on staff who can talk this all through with you."

"I'm not crazy," said Megan flatly.

"Of course not," said the Dean soothingly. "You're just tired. It happens to the best of us. But UHS has all sorts of resources for just this type of situation. Go down there, talk to someone, have a massage…. You'll feel much better for it. Have you heard about our new Wellness Wednesdays program?"

"It doesn't matter which day of the week it is," said Megan doggedly. "Or how many massages I have."

"Have you tried the whirlpool?" asked the Provost, but no one paid the slightest bit of attention to him.

"The fact remains that Professor Agnelli, in this very building, offered to alter his interpretation of school policy if I would see him socially and write him a memo justifying the same."

"You know," commented the Provost, sticking another decaf Hazelnut Crème into the coffee machine, "for someone who's overwrought, she expresses herself pretty articulately."

Agnelli cast the Provost a look that could be described as less than fond.

The Provost returned it with interest.

"Thank you, Chaz," the Dean said mildly. "You are always a source of invaluable insight. Ms…. I'm afraid I never caught your name."

"Milner."

"Ms. Milner, do you have anything with which to prove these allegations? You do realize that this is a serious charge you're attempting to levy, against a man whose reputation has always been above reproach."

Megan lifted her chin and met his eyes levelly. "I do. I have, in my inbox, a message from the Acting Dean acknowledging receipt of my memo, and expressing pleasure at the prospect of our future acquaintance."

"Arthur? This does sound serious."

"What proof are emails? A kindergartner knows how to forge them these days. An account name and a time signature are very easily changed. It is only to those of us of the older generation that these skills remain arcane."

"True, O King," said the Dean whimsically. "I must say, though, we seem to be going about this backwards. We really ought to have the prosecution before we have the defense. Ms. Milner, what exactly is it that you claim occurred between you and Professor Agnelli?"

A long whistle shattered the tense silence. A tall form loped into the room and slid an arm around Megan's waist.

"Looks like I got here just in time for the good bit," said Gabe.

He succeeded in one thing; for a moment Megan, the Dean, and Agnelli were all united in a common emotion. Annoyance.

"Is this a friend of yours, Ms. Milner?" demanded Agnelli in magisterial tones. He raised his brows at the Dean as though to say *I told you so*.

Megan slapped at Gabe's hand. "This is *not* a good time, Gabe!"

"Paul said you wanted to speak to me. Like now."

"He meant like *then*—over a day ago!"

"I've been busy."

The Dean might not recognize the face, but he certainly recognized the baseball cap. "I don't recall having invited you to join us at this meeting."

Gabe dismissed that omission with a benevolent wave of his hand. "That's okay. I'm not offended."

"Pity," said the Dean. "Before this turns into a complete zoo, I suggest we start at the beginning."

"Well," Gabe began. "The Law Review was kind of worried about old Cliff. Meggy had TFed for him, so—"

"Not you," bit off the Dean. "Ms. Milner?"

"As Mr. Lucas was saying, I was one of Mr. Walker's teaching fellows. Since I had worked closely with Mr. Walker, and was aware of the quality of his scholarship and the extenuating circumstances in his case, certain parties—"

"That would be me," interjected Gabe smugly.

"—deemed it best that I go speak to Dean Agnelli on his behalf. So I did."

"You see," broke in Agnelli hoarsely. "There's her motive, right there. I turned down her petition on behalf of Mr. Walker. She thinks that by blackening my reputation she can ensure Mr. Walker's continued employment. Or she simply wants to revenge herself on me for rejecting her arguments. It's as simple as that."

"Hmm," said the Dean, nodding thoughtfully. "I must say, that does make a great deal of sense. It has a nice poetic twist to it. There is, however, another angle that no one here has stopped to consider."

"And that would be?" asked Agnelli warily.

"The simplest point is often the most easily ignored. If you did, indeed, offer to trade your support for Mr. Walker in return for Ms. Milner's, er, personal charms, then wouldn't one have expected you to express some support for Mr. Walker?" The Dean spread his hands. "It's as simple as that. Occam's razor rides again."

The Provost drooped with disappointment.

The bill of Gabe's baseball cap wagged sagely. "He's got you there, Megs."

"In this case," protested Megan shrilly, "Occam's razor scrapes off the crucial part—the fact that *he* reneged on his side of the bargain!"

"Isn't it simpler just to admit that there never was a bargain?" asked the Dean gently. "Rather than push on with this farce?"

Megan's face contorted like Medea conjuring demons. "Is there *no* justice? Can't you tell he's lying? God, what do I have to do? Fling myself into a lake and float?"

"Not float," said the Dean apologetically. "Sink. You had to drown before you could prove you were right."

"Great," said Megan. "Just great."

"Sucks, doesn't it?" commented Gabe.

"It doesn't have to," said a new voice, from just behind him.

It wasn't a loud voice, but it captured the full attention of at least one member of the group.

"Hello, Arthur," said Marion Kucenik, smiling mistily at him across the room. "Are you surprised to see me?"

CHAPTER TWELVE

"This is that face, thou cruel Angelo,
Which once thou swor'st was worth the looking on;
This is the hand which, with a vowed contract
Was fast belocked in thine."
    -- V, i, 207-210

"I did but smile till now;
Now, good my lord, give me the scope of justice;
My patience here is touched. I do perceive
These poor informal women are no more
But instruments of some more mightier member
That sets them on."
    -- V, i, 233-238

The real author of *Legal Bodies* wore the same baggy clothes as the night before, but she wore them with a difference.

Her stooped shoulders had lifted; her spine had straightened; and she carried her head with a lift of the chin that could only be termed jaunty. Her hair was still coarse, her skin unmoisturized, but the gray fog that had surrounded her the night before had lifted. Her eyes, fixed on Agnelli, were bloodshot but clear, lit with an indefinable glow that had nothing to do with caffeine.

"Don't you recognize me, Arthur?" she asked. "Or have I changed that much?"

It was the first time Megan had seen Agnelli's composure crack. Shock trembled across his seamed face and carved a canyon where his mouth had been.

"Marion?" he mustered, before his voice failed him.

"Still the same," she said serenely, and the word seemed to contain a horrible sort of promise.

"Arthur?" the Dean prodded, poking the Acting Dean in the ribs. "Do you know this woman?"

The gesture broke Agnelli's paralysis. He shook himself, like a man trying to wake himself from a nightmare, his eyes still fixed on the woman across from him, the unhappy opposite of a mirage. "I... did."

"Did?" inquired the Dean.

"She was my graduate student. A very long time ago. But she never finished her dissertation."

"It's a common enough story," said the Dean genially. "Dissertations can be the very devil to finish. Even I started one back in the day."

"But I did finish," said Marion, smiling at Agnelli in a way that made the hairs on the back of Megan's arms prickle. "Didn't I, Arthur?"

Agnelli appeared entirely incapable of speech.

"If you finished your dissertation," asked the Dean, with the air of one reciting a well-rehearsed part, "where is your degree?"

"I never received it."

"A dissertation, but no degree?"

"Not only a dissertation, but a book."

"Will I have read it?"

"It doesn't have my name on it."

"Enough!" interjected Agnelli forcefully, breaking off the bizarre catechism. "Can't you see the poor woman is distraught?"

"Distraught… overwrought…." The Dean shook his head sadly. "This does seem to be our morning for mental disorders."

"A dissertation, but no degree; a book, without her name on it!" Agnelli slammed one fist into the opposite palm. "It's pure nonsense! I can introduce you to a beggar in the Square who claims to be the author of *War and Peace*, and another who thinks he's James Frey. Even they make more sense than she does."

"I don't know," said the Provost. "Sounds less like a claim than a riddle. I used to like those. What sort of box has no key, but many locks?" He looked expectantly around the group. "A box on the ears!"

"I don't think this is that sort of riddle, Chaz, although it's certainly mysterious. A dissertation but no degree… A book but no credit…." mused the Dean. "If someone stole your work and took it as her own, something ought to be done about."

"It wasn't stolen," said Marion. "It was a gift."

"And you're quite sure you're not James Frey?" said the Provost.

Marion seemed quite sure. "Shall I tell them how *Legal Bodies* came to be written, Arthur? Shall I tell them about us?"

"That's absurd!" snapped Agnelli. "It's all absurd!"

"I'd say," contributed Gabe, eying Marion's frumpy clothes with a connoisseur's eye, and marking her down as a bargain bin selection.

"Don't you find something a bit suspicious about this," countered Agnelli, "both these women turning up at once? I have many enemies…. The Federalist

Society, the Alliance of Anti-Feminists, the editorial staff at Harvard University Press. Bob Patterson at the Yale Law School would love to see me discredited. Clearly, someone has put these women up to this."

"Is this true?" asked the Dean gravely. "Are you acting on someone else's instructions?"

"I wouldn't put it that way," said Megan defensively.

"I'm sure you wouldn't. But someone did advise you."

"I spoke to one of the counselors at OCS. But that was all. Nobody else. And you certainly can't accuse the Office of Career Services of being in league with Yale!"

"What better way to infiltrate a school?" Agnelli seized on the notion, schooling his expression to the appropriate measure of outrage. "Think of the power, the influence they have at OCS, the access to students and information. He could sabotage our law firm placements for an entire year."

Nodding grimly, the Dean fixed Megan with a censorious stare. "And then he met you and came upon a whole new means of mischief. What was his name?"

"Bob Friar—but he certainly didn't put me up to this. I told you what happened. I went to Dean Agnelli on behalf of Cliff Walker, and—"

"But who told you about, er…." The Dean flapped a hand in Marion's direction in lieu of a name. "And how did she know to come here? It was Bob Friar, wasn't it?"

"Hey!" exclaimed Gabe belatedly. "I know that guy!"

"Bully for you," said the Dean briefly, not bothering to turn around.

"The man's a scumbag," said Gabe confidently. "You wouldn't believe some of the things he said to me."

"What sort of things?" asked the Provost.

"Well…." Gabe feigned reluctance. "He said some nasty things about Dean, accused you of letting the school go to ruin while you boozed it up, that sort of thing. Of course, I told him he was on crack."

"You shouldn't have," said the Dean.

"Hey." Gabe opened his hands wide in a gesture of self-deprecating benevolence. "I'm your biggest fan."

"Heaven preserve me from my enemies, then," muttered the Dean.

"He did tell me that he knew you," Megan said slowly. "He said you were old friends."

The Dean's face settled into grim lines. "I've never come face to face with the man. You, ladies, seem to have been the pawns in a clever hoax."

"I told you," said Agnelli.

"I suggest we get Friar over here, and then take matters from there." The Dean held up his cell phone, one of the sleek British models scarcely thicker than a credit card. "If you all wait here for just a moment, I'll call OCS and have them send him over."

Without pausing for an answer, he disappeared down the hall towards the back stairs.

"Bob Friar, a Yalie spy," the Provost shook his head bemusedly. "I should have guessed. Why else would he be lurking around our Ad Board meeting?"

"Hoping to sniff out scandal, no doubt," pronounced Agnelli darkly.

"Oh, he has plenty of that already," said Gabe. "You should have heard him ragging on the Dean last night. There was one story about the Dean and this woman who lives on Chauncy Street...."

"When did you see Mr. Friar?" Megan asked sharply.

"Last night. Paul and I were on our way back from...from a seminar on more effective modes of legal citation, and we ran into him."

"I should have known the moment I saw that hair," muttered the Provost, rearranging four strands of hair across an otherwise barren scalp. "What honest man wears a toupee?"

"What honest man tries to shift the blame for his own actions onto someone else?" countered Megan, looking defiantly at Agnelli. "Whoever Bob Friar is, it doesn't change the fact that you did what you did."

"We're not still on that, are we?" said the Provost. He checked his watch. "Does anyone have any idea how long they'll be? I have another meeting at eleven."

Agnelli regarded the Provost dispassionately. "It all depends on how long it takes Will to locate Friar."

"Did somebody say my name?"

An unruly mop of hair poked around the curve of the corridor, seemingly even more exuberant than the day before. In his orange bell-bottoms and afro, Bob Friar was dressed for the disco, and there was a distinct sashay to his stride as he minced into the Griswold Lounge.

"Hello, all," he said, smiling benignly around the group. "Megan... Gabe... Charles. Good to see you all again. I just stopped by to see how Cliff's hearing was going."

"You didn't get the Dean's call?" asked the Provost.

"Why are you even bothering to ask him?" demanded Gabe. "Can't you see he's a chronic liar? All that stuff he said about the Dean…."

"Don't you mean all that stuff you said about the Dean?" enquired Mr. Friar.

"See what I mean!" blustered Gabe, turning a slightly darker shade of tan beneath his baseball cap. "Total liar. That's not even his real hair!" Gabe reached out to pluck at one of the synthetic locks in illustration.

Never securely anchored, the entire edifice slid to the side. It slipped off a scalp that was not bare as expected, but covered with an expensively cut crop of black hair, gone silver at the sides like the facings on an expensive pen.

The forgotten wig dangled from Gabe's hand like a skinned poodle.

With an air of resignation, the Dean removed his massive glasses and folded them closed, revealing a pair of familiar pale-blue eyes, lightly feathered with lines.

"You," said the Dean to Gabe, tucking his glasses neatly away in the v-neck of his unfashionable two-tone sweater, "are becoming quite tedious."

Gabe didn't have a single thing to say. Neither did anyone else. In stunned silence, they stared at the alarming conjunction of the Dean's immaculately groomed head, the same head that appeared every year in the front of the Yearbook and the first page of all the law school bulletins, on top of Bob Friar's thrift shop clothes. Each circled in his own private gyre of unresting thought, remembering words better unsaid, deeds better undone, transgressions and omissions and grievances.

The Provost found his tongue first. He, after all, had nothing to regret, other than his choice of a second cup of coffee, which was already making him consider a trip to the little boys' room. Some things, however, trumped even an overfull bladder.

His eyes ran incredulously up the wide sweep of the orange bellbottoms to the red and yellow striped points of the Dean's collar. "Will? Is that really you?"

"The one and only," affirmed the Dean, adjusting the cuffs that stuck out beneath the white piping of his blue sweater. "What do you say, Chaz? Do the clothes really make the man?"

The Provost regarded the bellbottoms dubiously. "I hope this doesn't mean we have a new dress code. Platform shoes are hell on my arches."

"I don't think the alums would like it either," agreed the Dean. He turned to look at Agnelli, who stood still as stone just beyond the coffee machine, a little removed from the rest of the group. "Well, Arthur? What do you have to say? What do you think of my little sartorial experiment?"

"You weren't in Iraq."

"No, Arthur, I wasn't in Iraq. I've been here all this while, and I know exactly what has been going on. All of it."

The Acting Dean seemed to sag, like the House of Usher quivering on its foundations.

"Will…. I don't know what to say."

"That's a first," muttered the Provost.

"I don't know how to explain…."

"Don't say it to me. Say it to them. I'm not the one you wronged." The Dean paused a damning moment, regarding his long-time colleague with eyes from which all the false bonhomie had fled. For the first time since Megan had seen him, he looked his age, his cheeks graven with lines of old compromises and new betrayals. "The most."

Agnelli's face was equally grave, grave and ashen. "I never meant to betray your trust."

"My trust," the Dean said flatly. His eyes flicked briefly over to the two women. "You never *mean* any of it, do you, Arthur? Well, that's not an excuse any more. Ms. Milner made that point to me, and she was right. Willful ignorance only goes so far." Whether the willful ignorance was his or Agnelli's, he failed to specify. Moving on, he said briskly, "Our first order of business is righting an old wrong. *Legal Bodies.*"

The Provost made a slight, involuntary moue of distaste. He had never understood why that book got so much attention, even though his own book, *Observations on the Unintended Consequences of the Alternative Minimum Tax*, was clearly the worthier work. It had to be all because it had the word "bodies" in the title. As many publishers had noted, sex sold. The Provost resolved on the spot to title his next book *The Naked Tax Code*. Unless it would be more tasteful to call it *The Tax Code Unclothed...* he did have his wife and children to think about, after all, unlike Agnelli, who was encumbered by no such appendages.

"*Legal Bodies* has been out for over five years," protested Agnelli hoarsely.

"I would have let sleeping dogs lie. But you forced my hand, Arthur."

"What do you want me to do?"

"I want you to prepare a new edition of *Legal Bodies*, with a foreword acknowledging Ms. Kocenik's involvement in the researching and writing of it. Just how detailed you choose to make it, I leave to the two of you. But I expect to see her name on the cover. As co-author."

"But… my publisher…."

"Won't want to have to deal with any more allegations of plagiarism at HLS. We've had enough of those in the past few years already."

"Plagiarism?" broke in the Provost eagerly. "That is serious. If—"

The Dean silenced him with one upraised hand. "Arthur?"

Agnelli nodded, one abrupt tilt of his head. "As you wish."

"Not as I wish," said the Dean, with all the awful gravity of his office hanging from him like a crimson mantle. "As I require."

Agnelli's sunken eyes seemed to retreat even further under the overhang of his brow. "Understood."

"Next," said the Dean briskly, "we have the matter of Ms. Kucenik's employment. As she pointed out, she has finished her dissertation. Even had she not, an SJD has never been a prerequisite for being a member of the faculty of the law school. Few of us would be employed if it were. I'm sure you will all agree with me that her current employment at Cambridge Law is a sad waste of her obvious talents."

"What are you saying, Will?" asked the Provost warily. His lack of a higher degree had always been a bit of a sore point with him. He didn't even have a spare masters, or a youthful stint as a Fulbright recipient. It was a sad trial to him in the Faculty Lounge, where academic degrees were the designer labels of choice.

"I'm saying that we ought to offer Ms. Kucenik a position. Here."

"A new teaching position?" The Provost rounded on the Dean. "What are you thinking, Will? We're short on space as it is. We can't possibly hire an extra professor right now. Unless old Mortmain dies… but he's been hanging on for years. Still teaching, too." The Provost spared a moment to reflect sorrowfully on the plight of Mortmain's students. The man had been incomprehensible even when he did have all his teeth.

"I believe I have a solution to that," said the Dean, his gaze locking with Agnelli's.

Like the martyrs of old, Agnelli stood unflinching beneath the impact of each new stone, waiting without comment for his final sentence to be passed.

"You can't fire Mortmain, Will," said the Provost. "We've been over this before. He has tenure."

"Not Mortmain, Chaz. There are some things even tenure won't protect against. Arthur has spent years trying to persuade me of that. Murder, of course, but that went without saying. Plagiarism… that's a dodgier one. I'm sure we all agree in principle that plagiarism is wrong, but it's so hard to identify. There are so many gray areas. And then there is sexual misconduct."

With a rough edge of bitterness showing beneath his polished bonhomie, the Dean bared his teeth at Agnelli in a mockery of a smile. "That's Arthur's pet project. Isn't it, Arthur? For years now, he's been urging me to enforce those rules. And so I shall. Starting with him."

The Dean flung out one arm in a rhetorician's calculated gesture.

"What do you say, Megan? Shall I do unto Arthur as he would unto Cliff?"

CHAPTER THIRTEEN

"The very mercy of the law cries out
Most audible, even from his proper tongue
'An Angelo for Claudio, death for death!'
Haste still pays haste, and leisure answers leisure;
Like doth quit like, and Measure still for Measure."
     -- V, I, 406, 410-414

"I flatter myself that it has a nice, little poetic twist to it. And it will free up Arthur's office for Ms. Kucenik, which should make Chaz happy."

"You can't do that!" Marion grabbed at the Dean's sleeve. "You can't give me a job only to take one away from Arthur!"

"Can't I?" rejoined the Dean, shaking out his sleeve. "It seemed like quite a neat solution. An eye for an eye, and a scholar for a scholar. Measure for measure, as it were. Couldn't be tidier."

"But I want to work with *him*."

"Haven't you learned your lesson on that front?" demanded the Dean, with genuine surprise. "This is, after all, the man who coopted your doctoral thesis, turned it into a bestseller, and left you to languish in a library for seven years. The library, I might add, of a tenth rate educational institution."

"I don't care about that," vowed Marion. "Not anymore. Sure, it was hard at the beginning, realizing he had dumped me like that. You think I didn't realize it?"

"And you stayed anyway?" Megan wasn't sure which alternative was more alarming, simple obtuseness or blind devotion.

"I love him. I've always loved him. He's the foremost scholar of our generation. I would clean floors if it meant staying at the university with him."

"Yes, yes," said the Dean. "We have the picture. You would follow him to the ends of the earth and build a willow cabin at his gate."

Marion's brow wrinkled. "You mean like Tent City?" she asked, referring to the rough village of canvas that had sprouted in Harvard Yard during the living wage sit-in a few years back. Marion brushed aside the poetic notion of a love-in outside the law school. "I could have gone somewhere else, you know. I could have gotten another law firm job, or transferred to another school to finish my SJD. But I wanted to be near him, because I knew, someday, that we would have the chance to be together again. The way we were."

"Marion—" Agnelli's voice was thick with emotion, but Megan would have sworn it was more horror than affection.

"I'll take him back on whatever terms I can have him."

Under his breath, the Dean lightly whistled a familiar refrain. Megan recognized it as the first few bars of "Stand by Your Man."

Having been deprived of the Dean's arm, Marion pounced on Megan's. Her hands were as bony as the claws of Baba Yaga. "You know what he is."

"Now she does," interjected Gabe, not exactly sotto voce.

"You know the value of his work. Without him, the Center for Studies of Women in the Law will dissolve. There'll be no one to keep it up. Without him, the whole movement will have lost its center. There'll be no one to lead it. You may have won a battle, but you will have lost the war. There'll be no Feminist Legal Studies movement worth having. Please. Make them understand. They seem to listen to you."

If there was a slight touch of malice in that last line, it didn't seem the proper time to dwell on it.

The Dean tut-tutted. "Haven't you realized, Ms. Kucenik, that Ms. Milner is the last person you ought to appeal to? The woman he bullied and threatened and tried to discredit. She makes an unlikely choice of advocate."

"But the loss…" protested Marion, clinging to Megan's arm. "Think of it…."

Megan did. She thought of the bullying and the threatening, all the more dangerous for having been so subtle, presented with a maddening veneer of reason and the even more damaging illusion of free choice. She thought of Agnelli's hypocrisy in damning Cliff for the mildest form of what he intended to do himself. She thought of the terrifying prospect of rapine of the mind, the insidious intertwining of academic and sexual misconduct.

She thought of the cankered logic of his broken promises. Having made a meretricious bargain with her, Agnelli felt no compunction in failing to keep it. It was, after all, an invalid contract in the first place. His own conscience would be clear on those grounds, even if she had accepted it and performed her part in reliance upon it. It was legalism in its purist and most deadly form, justice as injustice, the slippery adherence to the letter of the law that gave lawyers a bad name and provided endless fodder for both populist activists and New Yorker cartoons.

"When our idols are shown to have clay feet," murmured the Dean, "we like nothing so much as to smash them."

"No," said Megan, and the abrupt word broke the silence.

She drew herself up and faced the Dean. By the coffee table, Agnelli, the center and focus of it all, seemed unimportant, peripheral, a smudge on the margins of her vision. There might have been no one present except for herself and the Dean, alone in the gray wasteland of the Griswold Lounge.

"Symbols can be powerful," she said slowly. "*He* taught me that, even before I came to HLS. And that's what it has to come down to in the end. It doesn't matter if the idol is really papier mache underneath the paint. He still stands for something important."

"Even as a hollow vessel?" enquired the Dean.

"It's like you said the other day, no matter who really wrote it, *Legal Bodies* has made a difference in the profession. If I discredit him, I discredit his work with him. And I can't be responsible for that." She couldn't resist adding, "No matter what I might think of his character."

"What about justice?" asked the Dean softly. "What about the rules?"

"A rule is only as good as the purpose it serves. We wouldn't have policy arguments in judicial opinions, otherwise. It would all just be pure textual construction."

"Some might not regard that as a drawback," the Dean commented.

Megan's expression betrayed what she thought about that school of legal thought and its purveyors, but she let it pass. "As for justice, it's almost never an absolute. Think of First Amendment jurisprudence, or eminent domain, or even evidence law—it's all about a balancing of conflicting interests. In this case, we could consider it not all that unlike a plea bargain. We know the criminal is guilty, but we allow him a lesser sentence in return for his doing something of use to the state. Isn't that the same situation we have here?" Megan concluded, running out of arguments and breath.

"That was a fascinating goulash of the first and second year curriculum you just served up for us. I'm glad to see we are still teaching something at the law school after all—even if the methods have been rather unconventional."

"Does that mean you won't have him dismissed?" interrupted the librarian impatiently.

The Dean looked a bit miffed at being derailed mid-oration. He had just been warming up. "Yes."

The Provost sought to assuage his disappointment by saying, half to convince himself, "It wouldn't have been good for the school to go through another scandal just now. Donations always go down in those situations, and this sort of thing in particular.... The female alums can be so touchy."

"They're called alumnae, Chaz. Alumna in the singular," the Dean said absently, his eyes fixed on Agnelli. "And, in the end, I believe we've just meted out a worse punishment to Arthur than any under the Rules. A dismissal is a finite thing. It happens and then it's over. Whereas Arthur has to go through the rest of his career knowing that we know what he really is. Even worse than that, *he* knows what he really is. And he'll never, ever be able to escape that. Will you?"

Agnelli's eyes looked like coals, sunken into the taut skin of his face. "No."

The Dean's studied calm cracked. "Why, Arthur?" he demanded. "Why did you have to force us to this? We gave you every opportunity to back down. All you needed to do was admit to having had that conversation with Megan—you could even have claimed that she had misunderstood you. Anyone would have believed you. Even *she* might have believed you. You would have believed yourself in time. You did the last time. We could have gone on just as we had before." The Dean scrubbed a hand through his immaculate hair. "Why did you have to cheat?"

Agnelli smiled mirthlessly. "If I didn't admit it, it never happened."

"And if you didn't keep your half of the bargain with her, it never happened either. Just the way your liaison with Marion never happened once she was safely out of the way. Is that it?" asked the Dean roughly.

"Something like that."

"Christ, Arthur!"

"That," said Agnelli very slowly, "is precisely the problem. It is very wearing always being the public conscience."

"You might have tried looking after your own instead. No one asked you to play moral compass for the world at large."

"Didn't you?"

Agnelli didn't elaborate. He simply left, following his new colleague out of the room with all the dignity of an Old Testament prophet descending his mount.

The Dean stared after him, dyspeptic with half-digested arguments that could not be uttered. There was something terribly un-Dean-like about shouting after a man's retreating back, and Arthur had taken full advantage of that fact.

He didn't miss a trick.

The Dean's unpleasant thoughts were interrupted by the sound of a masculine howl. He emerged from his reverie to the gratifying sight of Gabe hopping on one foot, emitting yips and yelps of pain, while Megan glowered at him, with both hands on her narrow hips.

"Don't touch me," she declared fiercely, looking more than ready to visit injury upon whichever other part of Gabe's anatomy might conveniently come within reach. "We are officially over."

"As to that," interrupted the Dean, with a most unacademic glint in his eye, "you, Mr. Lucas, are also officially over."

For the first time, Gabe began to look a bit uncomfortable. "Um, you know, all that stuff I said before—I didn't mean it."

"Stuff is the word for it," replied the Dean dryly. "To which stuff were you referring?"

"All of it!"

"Including that fascinating confidence about cheating on your 1L exams?"

"But it wasn't just me! A whole bunch of people did it! I—"

"*You* are the only one who has admitted to it. Twice, now. Would you care to confess a third time, just to round it out? Ah, well, two should do nicely. Thank you so much for making the Ad Board's job that much easier. Cheating, Mr. Lucas, merits immediate expulsion. Under any interpretation of the Rules."

"But—you can't do this to me! I'm on the fucking Law Review!"

"That, Mr. Lucas, can only protect you so far. Considering that you attained your place on the Law Review by means of unfairly obtained exam scores, forgive me if I fail to be suitably impressed."

"I'll sue!"

"On what grounds?" The Dean herded Gabe inexorably backwards, towards the open elevator. "I would advise you to prepare to find another line of work. Junk bonds, I think. That should suit you to a tee. Good-day, Mr. Lucas. I look forward to not seeing you around campus."

With one efficient motion, the Dean bumped Gabe back through the open elevator doors. The doors slid neatly shut on Gabe's outraged face.

"That," declared the Dean with great satisfaction, as he turned to face Megan, "felt good. I should expel students more often."

His grin faded as he took in Megan's frozen expression.

"Not you, of course," he amended, quirking an eyebrow.

"Why did you do it?" she asked, watching him with a furrow between her brows. "If you knew what Dean Agnelli was doing, why didn't you just reveal yourself, and stop it? Why the whole masquerade in the first place?"

The Dean clasped his hands lightly behind his back, strolling meditatively back and forth across the shallow strip of space between the elevator and the lounge.

"I do apologize for the necessity of deceiving you," he said, in a voice so rich with regret that Megan nearly failed to notice that he had neatly skipped over the central question. "I know I gave you a very bad forty-eight hours by letting this all go on as I did. But if I had just barged in as myself, Arthur would have simply denied everything—and you would never have come to me for help in the first place."

Megan remembered her earnest heart-to-hearts with Bob Friar, and grimaced in distaste. Her tergiversations, Cliff's groveling, Gabe's pandering.... "You must have found us all pretty pathetic."

"Not pathetic. Gallant." There was something in the way he looked as he said it that made the color rise in Megan's cheeks. "That's a rare quality these days. Especially here. There are very few people willing to take the time to tilt at windmills."

"Naïve dreamers, you mean."

"Visionaries," corrected the Dean. "Hasn't law school taught you that it's all in the twist of a word?"

Megan wordlessly shook her head.

"And it's an even rarer visionary who is willing to let circumstances anchor her dreams to the imperfections of realities. What you did, in standing up for Arthur, was one of the more noble gestures I have seen—in a career that's gone on longer than you've been alive," the Dean added ruefully.

"It wasn't noble," protested Megan. "It was practical."

"There you have it," said the Dean. "The very highest kind of nobility. By demanding Arthur's immediate expulsion, you could have had the personal satisfaction of remaining pure to your principles in their ideal abstract form. Instead, you sacrificed your own peace of mind for the greater good of your own chosen cause. You thought of realities instead of abstractions, and you served your goals better for it."

"It stills seems upside down," said Megan.

"Welcome to the real world," said the Dean, so drolly that Megan couldn't help but smile in response. With a slightly inquiring tilt to his brows, he added, "Now that you've sent that distressing young man packing—"

Megan winced. Of all the day's manifold trials, having her dating misdeeds dragged to light shouldn't have bothered her, but it did. More than anything else, it stung to be found guilty of such poor taste.

"—I'm assuming your evening tonight will be free."

Engaged in her own private orgy of self-flagellation, it took Megan a moment for the meaning of his words to sink in.

"I didn't have any plans with Gabe anyway," she said stupidly. "Not for a long time. We fizzled out a long time ago."

"Good," said the Dean cheerfully. "Then how would you feel about sharing a drink with me? To discuss the future of the women's studies program, of course."

"Of course," echoed Megan, absurdly gratified by the invitation. After all that had passed, all her missteps and meanderings, all the madness of the past few days, it was a powerful relief to know that she hadn't discredited herself entirely in his eyes, that he thought her worth knowing, Dean though he was, that he wanted to share a drink, and discuss the future of academia. That he thought her noble and gallant.

For all his age, he was still a very attractive man.

The thought acted on Megan like a wash of icy water straight from the Charles.

"I hope," said the Dean, "that you will consider me as much of a friend as you did foolish Bob Friar. My clothes may have changed, but nothing else."

"A friend," repeated Megan. There was nothing sketchy about it on its face. Friend, advisor, confidante…. It was only her own thoughts that had betrayed her, and the bizarre events of the past few days, putting groundless suspicions in her head. The Dean was worlds too worldly and sophisticated for that, even if he did think of her in that way, which he didn't. Even if she thought of him in that way, which she wouldn't.

"A good friend," the Dean confirmed, smiling warmly down at her. "So… tonight?"

Pasting a sickly social smile on her face, Megan forced suitably polite words through her lips. It was all in her own head… it was all in her own head…. "Would you excuse me for a second? I just have to make a quick call to check my plans."

The Dean spread one hand in a gracious gesture. "Certainly. Take all the time you need. I'll be in my office." He favored her with a comradely grin. "I know you know where it is."

Slipping into the relative privacy of the stairwell, Megan dug her cell phone out of the bottom of her bag and dialed information. It took them only a moment to connect her to the number she wanted.

"Hello? Is this the Yale Law School Admissions Office? My name is Megan Milner, and I'd like to request a transfer application…."

AUTHOR'S NOTE

In the winter of 2005, my 2L year of law school, I trudged downtown to Boston through the winter slush to see a production of *Measure for Measure* put on by the Actors Shakespeare Project.

At the time, I harbored vague notions of writing a re-take of *Measure for Measure*, set in 16th century Italy. In my other life—my non-law school life—I was a lapsed Renaissance historian and a published historical fiction writer. I'd always been fascinated by the personal relationships in *Measure for Measure*, particularly that vexed question of whether or not Isabella went willingly to the Duke in the end. As many critics have pointed out, we hear nothing more from her lips at that point. It's all conjecture. The romantic in me liked to believe that *Measure for Measure*'s ending was fundamentally a happy one, in which Isabella's rigid notions of right and wrong were forced to bow to a realization of the power of human emotion. I'd meant to write it as a love story.

In the meantime, I was also plotting an entirely different sort of book, a Waugh-esque satire set at HLS, to be written, should the powers that be agree, as my 3L project. I was itching to write about the vagaries of the 2L job hunt, the strange subculture of the law journals, and the odd advent of a law school sorority. I had plenty of material to mock; what I lacked was a plot.

Watching the ASP production of *Measure for Measure*, those two projects came together with an audible click. Where better than a law school to explore the questions of law and justice raised in *Measure for Measure*? The transition from Duke to Dean was almost too easy, and it seemed only fitting that, in the modern context, the spiritual advisor, the friar, should be replaced by the career counselor.

I would like to emphasize that the events in the novel are drawn solely from Shakespeare and do not reflect anything that occurred during my tenure at HLS (with the sole exception of the free coffee). While I borrowed the physical structure of HLS, all organizations and characters are entirely fictional.

This book reflects a great debt to the non-fictional folks at HLS: to Amy Gutman, for her support and advice and for her tireless efforts to bring law and literature together at Harvard; to Professor Hay, for supervising my project; to the Winter Writing Program, for giving me the time in which to write it; to my classmates, especially Emily, Weatherly, and Elina, for making everything more amusing; and, of course, to Dean Kagan, for the free coffee.

ABOUT THE AUTHOR

A graduate of Yale University, Lauren Willig received a graduate degree in history from Harvard and a JD magna cum laude from Harvard Law, while authoring a bestselling series of historical fiction set during the Napoleonic Wars. She practiced as a litigator at a law firm in New York before deciding that book deadlines and doc review don't mix. She now writes full time.

Made in the USA
Lexington, KY
03 February 2012